"Winston? Oh, my God, Winston! I knew you'd come. I was waiting. I knew!" The outburst went on, slightly garbled with tears, as weight slammed against his body.

He grabbed for it, lest it fall. Or he did. Arms clung to him, around his neck, as breasts fit into him in a familiar, completely natural way. His arms lowered enough to find their place at the curve of waist just below his as his foot scooted, allowing room for the smaller foot sliding in between his.

The drill was embedded in him. As much of his naval training had been. Came to him with ease. Until Emily lifted her head, gazed into his eyes and planted her mouth against his.

Lips pursed tightly closed, he stood there, eyes open.

And waited for her to figure out that the man she'd known and loved no longer existed.

* * *

THE PARENT PORTAL:
A place where miracles are made

Dear Reader,

Welcome to The Parent Portal—a place where miracles are made for those struggling to have children. A place where the professionals trying to make the magic happen might find a miracle or two of their own. So come with me inside the doors of The Parent Portal, a privately owned fertility clinic where biology matters. People here understand that donors are more than science—and they arrange legally binding agreements that provide both parties with "the right to know." The right to know if a child is born. To know the child is loved and safe. The right to find your biological child if you have a burning need to do so.

Or the right to have a child with your soldier husband's sperm when he dies in battle.

So much in the world is uncertain, but at The Parent Portal, you can be sure that people come first, love matters and miracles can happen.

Having the Soldier's Baby is my eighty-ninth novel with Harlequin and I can promise you an intense, emotional ride!

I love to hear from readers! You can find all of my social media at tarataylorquinn.com!

Happy reading!

TTQ

Having the Soldier's Baby

Tara Taylor Quinn

HARLEQUIN® SPECIAL EDITION

Recycling programs
for this product may
not exist in your area.

ISBN-13: 978-1-335-57392-6

Having the Soldier's Baby

Copyright © 2019 by TTQ Books LLC

Printed in U.S.A.

Having written over eighty-five novels, **Tara Taylor Quinn** is a *USA TODAY* bestselling author with more than seven million copies sold. She is known for delivering intense, emotional fiction. Tara is a past president of Romance Writers of America and is a seven-time RWA RITA® Award finalist. She has also appeared on TV across the country, including *CBS Sunday Morning*. She supports the National Domestic Violence Hotline. If you need help, please contact 1-800-799-7233.

Visit the Author Profile page
at Harlequin.com for more titles.

To all of those who've struggled to have a family...
may your hearts be filled with love.

Chapter One

Dear Emily,

Forgive my familiarity. We've never met and yet I feel as though I know you. You will be receiving formal notification, but I couldn't leave it at that. The decision has been made to officially pronounce Winston's death. This will award you the death benefits and pension you deserve, and yet somehow, I sense that isn't what matters to you.

As Winston's immediate superior I could go on about the standout soldier he was. But during this last tour... I walked into the trap with him. Ahead of him. I unknowingly led him to his eventual death. He saved my life. And we spent days in hiding together. Perhaps I am being selfish, but I need you to know that you are all that kept us alive. His talk

*of you. His love for you. His belief that that kind
of love was real.*

*In any event, it's been two years since he left to
find water for us and never came back. Two years
since I was discovered by friendly forces. Two years
of trying to understand why I am here and he is
not. He had everything to live for.*

*Please know that for the rest of my life, I am
here for you, a willing servant, pledging to have
your back or do whatever I can for you, no matter what...*

A signature followed. Contact information. Emily
couldn't see any of it through her tears. She wadded up
the letter and threw it across the room, half watching as it
hit the wood blinds open to the California sunshine outside her living room window. *Their* living room window.

Dressed in black pants that hugged her ankles, a loose
cream-colored sheath, and a short black-and-cream three-
quarter-sleeve open sweater, with three-inch black stilet-
tos, she tried to pretend that this day was like any other,
that she hadn't been up all night, that she was prepared
for the meeting she would be leading that morning in the
largest conference room of the LA marketing firm she'd
been with since college.

The forty-five-minute drive north might have been
preparation enough if she hadn't spent the past twelve
hours vacillating between grief that cut the air out of her
lungs and an anger that was equally debilitating.

In the ten years she'd been with the firm, she'd never
called in sick. She'd been at work when officials had
come to her two years before to inform her that Winston
was missing in action in Afghanistan. She'd remained

in her office, mostly comatose, but there, until the end of the day, but had put in for a couple of vacation days before she'd left.

She usually scheduled vacation for birthdays and anniversaries.

And this?

What was it really, but a formality? Something everyone around her assumed?

Good news, even, as it released benefits to her that she didn't already have.

She didn't need them.

She needed Winston.

Staring out the blinds, at the grass that she kept carefully manicured just as Winston had, she let the sun's bright glint partially blind her for a moment or two as she tried to look past it to find some kind of direction.

For two years she'd refused to believe the love of her life was dead. Winston wouldn't leave her on earth alone. They'd promised when they were fourteen that they'd be there for each other for the rest of their lives. And at fifteen, when they'd proclaimed their romantic love. And again at twenty-two, when they'd stood in front of an entire town's worth of family and friends and made the vow publicly.

For two years, she'd refused to believe.

For two years she'd been alone, living in an emotional freezer, waiting.

No answers appeared in the brightness outside her window. Stars and yellow-lined pink smears dotted her vision as she moved toward her purse and keys. She had to get to the office.

She wasn't dead, and work was the life she had.

Almost at the front door, Emily glanced toward the living room. Tearing up again, she went back, picked up the wadded paper, carefully smoothed it. Carried it out to the car with her. Drove all the way to LA with it on her lap.

She parked in her designated spot five minutes ahead of schedule. Dropped her keys in their pocket in her purse. And very carefully, she picked up the letter, folded it and slid it in her wallet.

Emily wasn't 100 percent on board with her plan a month later when she presented herself at the fertility clinic in town. Her heart was all there, 150 percent. Her body, the same.

But her mind…wasn't totally convinced she hadn't lost it.

"Let's head back to my office," Christine Elliott, the clinic's founder and manager, said as she collected Emily from the large and oddly calming waiting room. Instead of sitting in seats placed close together, forcing patients to face each other, the comfortable armchairs were arranged in separate areas, only two to four per grouping, with large floral arrangements separating them. Healing tones of new age music played, and the wall art, with predominant shades of purple, was somehow comforting.

The air was infused with a hint of lavender. She recognized the scent immediately only because, in her attempts to survive over the past couple of years, she'd gone through a phase of relying heavily on aromatherapy.

And, okay, still dabbed her wrists with pure lavender oil on occasion.

She'd taken up carrying peppermints with her at all times, too—just in case they really did promote calm and mental clarity.

As they reached the door bearing Christine's placard

at the end of the inner hallway, Emily pulled an individually wrapped little white circle out of her pocket and slipped it into her mouth. Fresh breath was always good.

In a short flowered summer dress, Christine could have been heading out for a day of shopping and lunch with friends. Emily liked that. Just…it felt better entering her office for "that" conversation with a woman who looked like shopping and lunch, rather than austerity.

Not one who'd ever really spent tons of time contemplating her wardrobe once she'd purchased clothes—figuring she did the work in the store so whatever was in her closet had already passed inspection—Emily had troubled herself for most of her shower time that morning, trying to determine what to wear. Would she do better if she appeared casual, like she was fully sane and prepared to calmly bring a child into the world all alone?

Or would businesslike and competent serve her better?

Her white capris and short black top with jeweled thongs didn't seem to matter a whit as she took a seat on the couch Christine indicated for their meeting.

The first time she'd been in that room—the only other time she'd been there—she and Winston had been shown to the two leather-bottomed seats in front of Christine's massive light wood desk. She'd liked sitting there. The woman's desk looked like something out of an upscale trinket shop, with everything carefully placed to show it off in its best light. To tempt you to want to own it. Angels in various forms. A china horse. Florals and a small colorful metal heart sculpture.

The couch, also light-colored and leather, faced the chair Christine had landed on. Emily had nowhere to look but in the other woman's eyes.

"You asked to speak with me specifically," Christine

opened the conversation. No "How have you been?" Or "Nice to see you."

Emily nodded, her light blond hair loose and straight around her shoulders. She used to curl it. Pull it back in clips. It all seemed like too much trouble these days.

"You were behind me in school...what, a couple of years?" she asked inanely, panicked for a second as she grappled with the reality of what she was doing. Christine had never attended parties or been a part of any crowd that Emily knew of, but she'd recognized her when she and Winston had visited the clinic.

He hadn't remembered her.

"Three years. I was a freshman your senior year."

"You used to leave during lunch. The McDermott Street door was down the hall from my locker and I'd see you..."

Only seniors had been allowed to leave for lunch.

"You always left alone..."

She'd wondered about it, in the way you're curious about something in the moment and then forget about it. It hadn't been any of her business.

And still wasn't.

"My grandmother was diabetic and needed an insulin shot," Christine said, not seemingly at all put out by Emily's rudeness. Or the unprofessional and inappropriate topic of conversation.

"You were, what, fourteen?"

Christine's short dark hair barely touched her shoulders as she shrugged. "I wanted to help, thought it was cool and seriously didn't mind doing it. Gram said Gramps hurt when he did it. Besides, she always had a great lunch ready for me when I got there."

Still...she'd been fourteen. A kid. Missing out on all of

the gossip and drama in the lunchroom. And the friendships that formed or solidified because of them.

Not to say that Christine hadn't had a slew of friends. Emily had no idea who Christine had known.

"I was sorry to hear about Winston." The compassion in Christine's brown eyes came close to undoing her. And focused her, too. Finally.

"That's why I'm here," she said, sitting upright on the couch, nothing at her back. Because that's how it was going to be. "Labwerks contacted me… I actually forgot to pay my yearly storage fee…"

Christine could have jumped in as Emily faltered. Instead, she sat silently, that warm look still in her gaze.

"They asked if I wanted them to discard Winston's sperm…"

The vial had been taken as part of an initial testing process when he and Emily first visited Elliott Fertility Clinic. They'd been trying to have a child for over a year with no success. Low motility had been ruled out. As had any other obvious reasons for an inability to procreate. They'd been given the option to keep trying naturally, with some hormonal help, or consider artificial insemination. Because they'd both just turned thirty and figured they had time, they'd opted to go the natural route for a while longer, but had paid to have Winston's sperm stored just in case.

"So what can I do for you?" Christine's question came quietly. More of a boost than a push. Like she was helping Emily do what she'd come to do, not forcing her to get on with it.

"I've become obsessed by an idea I had and I want your opinion before I allow myself to seriously consider it."

"Why me? I'm not a counselor— Though, as you

know, we have a couple of top-rate ones on staff, and I'd be happy to refer you…"

Emily shook her head. Maybe a counselor was what she needed but it wasn't what she wanted. Not at that point, anyway.

"I want your opinion."

"My degree is in health management. I founded the clinic, I run it, but the work that we do…that's the fabulous doctors and their teams, not me."

"When we met with you before…it was clear to me… you aren't in this as a business. You're here because you care about people."

With a silent nod, Christine acknowledged the truth of the remark.

"And…you understand that sometimes, for some people, the need to have a family, by whatever means, overrides most everything else…"

"Whatever *legal* means…" Christine said slowly, her look more assessing. "What are you considering?"

"Nothing illegal." Emily tried to smile and chuckle. She choked instead. And when Christine brought her a bottle of water, she took down half of it. "I'm sorry."

Taking the seat next to her on the couch, Christine turned to her. "I'm happy to listen."

Chapter Two

Emily rambled for what seemed like an hour. She just talked. Unburdening herself of myriad thoughts. Relaying arguments that played out in her head. Releasing a little bit of the panic that had become an almost-constant companion over the past month. She wasn't looking for healing. For therapy. Truth was, she wasn't sure what she was looking for. Permission maybe.

She wanted some kind of professional response from the health care manager, as though such a response would validate the seemingly unstoppable urge to have herself inseminated.

The clock on the wall said only about ten minutes had passed when she finally fell silent.

"You have the legal right to use your husband's sperm." Christine's response sounded professional. And maybe more, too.

She didn't need the other woman's pity. She had so much of that coming at her she was almost buried in it.

"Everyone I know is feeling sorry for me," she blurted. "I'm attempting to prevent myself from sinking into the pool they're creating and letting it drown the life out of me. And yet is it fair to bring a child into the world because I'm drowning in grief?"

"Is that why you'd be doing it? Because of the grief?"

It was obvious, wasn't it? That's what everyone would think. Would assume. Including her.

"When I met with you before it seemed to me that you and Winston were equally determined to have a child. That it was something you both needed in equally intense measure."

"It was!" Why would the woman be going back there at this point in time? That dream, that life, was over.

"And your desire to be a mother, to raise a family, do you think that died with your husband?"

"Of course not. If it had, having a child wouldn't assuage the grief now, would it?" She heard the sarcasm in her tone. Was ashamed of it. And kind of relieved to know that she had fight left in her, too.

Christine stared at her. Expecting her to get something?

"My mother died when I was ten, trying to have the sibling I so badly wanted, the son my father wanted," Christine stated a few moments later. "She was forty at the time. Because my father worked eighty hours a week, he left me with my grandparents…"

"The grandmother who was diabetic." Emily's turmoil settled, desperation eased for a second, as she saw again the high school girl leaving at lunchtime.

Christine nodded. "Other things happened that don't

bear going into right now, but ultimately, at twenty-two, I was alone, without any close family, and only the money left to me from my mother's life insurance policy."

And here Emily had been wallowing in her own pity. Compassion spread through her instead.

"I'd spent the previous twelve years fighting off grief, eschewing all the pity, desperately grasping sometimes, and there I was, a college graduate with a degree in health management, thinking I'd go on to med school as my mother had…"

"Your mother was a doctor? Here in Marie Cove?" Their little town wasn't all that well known, had no public beach access, but though it had only been incorporated for a couple of decades, it had been around more than a century and had enough of a population that not everyone knew one another.

"A pediatrician," Christine said. "Children were her life."

And she died trying to give birth to one. Emily wasn't sure where Christine was going with this, but for the first time since she'd received word that her husband had been declared legally dead, Emily felt a sense of…calm. And maybe a wee bit of strength, too.

"I had a choice to make," Christine said. "I could take that money, leave Marie Cove, start a new life for myself, a family of my own, or I could stay here in the town where I was born, in the home where I grew up, and use my mother's money to honor her life and the importance of children to families. To make it easier for women like her, and others, too, to have the children they need to feel complete. To give couples that chance."

The fertility clinic.

Emily wanted to take the other woman's hand. To

thank her somehow, though nothing in her life was any different than it had been moments ago. "What happened to your father?"

"He met a woman in LA, ten years older than me, twenty younger than him, remarried, had his son. And another daughter, too. They never asked me to live with them, but honestly, even if they had, I'd have chosen to stay with my grandparents."

"Do you see them? Your dad and his family? Your half brother and sister?"

"Once or twice a year. For an hour or so over a meal, usually. I never got along with his new wife. Probably somewhat my fault. But on the other hand, he never tried all that hard to bridge the gap."

Certain that there was a lot more Christine wasn't saying, Emily thought over what she had said. Searching for its application to the current situation.

"You're worried about the morality of using Winston's sperm when he isn't here to father his child. Or have any say in whether or not he has a fatherless child in the world."

Christine's statement hit home. Hard. "I didn't say that."

"You kind of did."

Not in so many words...but she'd rambled a lot and... "I guess that's part of it," she said, clasping her hands together in her lap, slumping some, too, but still not leaning back against the couch. "Is it fair to the child? To bring him or her into a single-parent home?"

"You know these are questions only you can answer."

But that didn't mean she liked that truth.

"A lot of people have disagreed with choices I've made in my life," Christine continued. "One of them was choosing to use my mother's money to build this clinic when I could have gone on to med school, or been a lawyer, or had any other life. But for me, this clinic is a part of her, and using my life to keep her legacy alive, to actually be able to give other people what she wanted most—the chance to have babies—this was my right choice. I'm happier today than I've been since I was ten and lost her."

Emily believed her.

"You have to make your right choice," Christine's words fell softly between them. "I could tell you what I think, or give you pros and cons, but you've done a pretty stellar job of arguing both sides all on your own."

No disputing that one.

"You know the paperwork you and Winston signed when you started with us gives you permission for the use of his sperm."

She knew. Of course she knew. Her, and only her. That had been important to them.

"How do I know this is the choice he'd have wanted me to make?"

Therein was the crux of her self-torture. They'd never talked about one of them carrying on without the ever. It hadn't been an option for them. Or a possibility she'd ever considered.

Hard to believe she'd ever been that naive.

"He's not here, Emily. You think my mother would choose for me to be living alone in her parents' home, dedicating my life to work? You think she'd choose for me to never have babies of my own?"

When she put it that way…not likely.

"You're young. You've got a lot of years to have kids."

"I'm childless by choice." The brightly dressed woman

smiled as she looked around her office. "This is my life. There's no doubt in my mind that I made the right choice. And my point to you is…just because grief plays a part in your choice, that doesn't mean it's reactionary, and therefore invalid."

Emily considered that for a moment before replying. "I've known since I was a teenager that I was going to be the mother of Win's kids someday. I knew I'd have a career, that I'd be someone professionally, that that was important to me, but being the mother of his kids, being his wife, mattered more than anything else."

"Do you still feel that way?"

Emily smiled and teared up a bit, too. "I think that's pretty obvious, huh?"

Christine shrugged.

"I'm going to do this."

No judgment came from the other woman. No sense that she was doing the right or wrong thing. That she'd made the choice Christine thought she should make. Or hadn't.

But she felt a kinship with her.

"I've got the ability to have my husband live on, even after his death, to bring parts of him to life, to give him descendants. I can raise his children and love them as much as we both wanted to. I know his views on pretty much every aspect of raising children…we talked end-lessly about schooling, about discipline—even eating habits we'd allow. And not allow. It's crazy-sounding, but Winston and I…we were just meant to be. And our family was meant to be, too."

She wasn't rambling anymore. Wasn't lost in the not-knowing. She and Winston had talked over every detail of child raising, of investing, of career plans, vacationing, homeownership, pet acquiring—but they'd never once talked about one of them not being there.

They'd never discussed death.

She knew how he'd thought about telling his children about sex, but had no idea what he'd think of her using his sperm to have his baby after he died.

So she couldn't make this decision based on him. She was the only one left. The choice was hers alone.

The first big decision she'd ever made completely alone.

"It might not take," she said aloud, still a bit shaky as a whole new set of worries came upon her. "This might all have been for nothing if I can't get pregnant."

"Nothing in your tests showed you to be infertile."

"I know, but…"

"If nothing else, insemination gives you a better shot," Christine said, more distant and professional now than she'd been. "If you're still unsure, or thinking it might be better if it didn't work, if you're looking for an out…"

"I'm not!" She stood, and Christine followed suit. "I want this child more than anything…"

Christine's smile was a surprise. But not as much of one as the hug the other woman reached over and gave her.

"I know," the health director said. "And now you do, too."

Chapter Three

"My name is Winston Hannigan. I am a chief petty officer first class." He rattled off his serial number. "I was deployed as a sand sailor under the Individual Augmentee Combat program two years and four months ago. For the past two years I have been living with the enemy."

They could shoot him dead on the spot, lying there on the ground, hands behind his head. Part of him wished they would. Most of him wished it.

They were US Army. A sergeant and a private, based on the uniform markings. Both heavily armed.

As he'd been before they'd stripped him of his guns and ammo and the blade in his boot. His US-issued boot, with holes in the sole, worn with his pale gray kuchi dress and loose pants.

No one from the United States was going to believe he was still on their side. Most days he questioned it himself.

The string of curse words that followed sounded unbelievably good to him—issued as they were in his native tongue. Even the word *traitor* attached at the end of it made him want to weep with relief. It had been so long since he'd heard American English.

He wasn't a traitor. Hadn't betrayed his country's secrets. But he'd done what he'd done. There was no undoing it. And no way to live with it, either.

He just wanted it over. Was ready to die, just like his heart and soul had already done. Winston Hannigan, married naval officer with a future at home, had been buried in the Afghan desert ages ago.

Hungry, thirsty, tired, Winston didn't argue when he was hauled up roughly, his shoulders half coming out of his sockets. Didn't care at all that the servicemen restrained him and threw him in the back of their off-road vehicle. He'd been on the road for three days with a goal that could go one of two ways: he'd get out of the desert or die in it.

The way he figured, that Jeep, the excruciating jars as it bumped along at top speeds, was helping him reach his goal. Maybe both ways.

The actual insemination wasn't painful. In a room with mood-enhancing new age music playing and the lighting low, other than the small bright light positioned for the doctor, and the lavender candle she'd brought burning not too far away, it was all over while she was still mentally preparing for the ordeal. She tried to doze while waiting the appropriate time before she could get up and go home. Thought about what she'd have for dinner—some kind of treat to celebrate.

Couldn't land on anything.

Wasn't happy about that.

She did a lot of math in her head. Financial reports,

estimating amounts of money needed per year to raise a child, adding in incidentals for vacations and the unforeseen, college account deposits and even possible competition fees if he or she was into sports or dancing.

She counted months. If the insemination took, she'd have a March baby. Counted days, fourteen of them, until she would know if the process was successful. She could take a home pregnancy test earlier than that, but according to Dr. Miller false positives were fairly common any earlier due to low hormonal counts.

Salad ended up being dinner—she didn't have much of an appetite. And she didn't call anyone. Her mother, a widow living with Emily's divorced brother in San Diego, helping him raise his two kids, would insist on driving up. And her friends… Most of them had either moved away or faded off. She didn't go out anymore, not since Winston went missing. Most of the people she used to spend time with were other couple friends with families of their own now, leaving her the odd one out—and she worked eighty hours a week and didn't relish spending even more time with the people there.

Another math problem to work through. Getting as much work done in fewer hours. She couldn't spend eighty hours in the office every week once a baby came. Child care funds had already been calculated. Multiple times. There was a day care in an office building not far from hers. The Bouncing Ball's LA branch. Mallory Harris, the owner, was a client at the clinic—and expecting a baby of her own around Christmastime. Christine Elliott had introduced them.

If all went well, they'd be pregnant at the same time. Pregnant. She could be. Winston's baby could already be forming inside her.

Math. Numbers. Focus.

Wednesday, June 12. Insemination day.

Conception Day?

Two years, four months and three days since she'd seen the father.

Hugging Winston's pillow, Emily cried herself to sleep that night.

"I did things."

Sitting on a worn blue couch, elbows on his khaki-covered knees, hands steepled at the fingers, Winston tried to help the naval therapist understand. Though he'd been back in the States for more than a week, in San Diego for three days, he didn't feel any different than he had bumping around helplessly in the back of a military Jeep in the Afghan desert. He'd murdered his soul there. Nothing was going to change that.

"You're a hero to your country." The woman's soft tones bounced off his eardrums like the buzz of an irritating fly. "What you did saved lives. And what you've brought back to us will save even more."

He didn't need to be told the facts. He knew them. Was wearing the ribbons he'd earned above his right pocket. He'd put country and his fellow comrades before soul. Had made very clear decisions—for very clear reasons. He'd come up with the plan on his own. Had implemented it without telling anyone, knowing that if he'd spoken up, he'd have been told not to act.

His plan had succeeded. Beyond his expectations. He hadn't counted on surviving.

"My wife believes I'm dead. I wish to leave it that way." An unusual request, but not impossible. He was informing on a terrorist cell. He could request a new identity. Keep anyone who knew him by his former identity out of it.

Not that they were really in any danger. No one in the sect he'd joined knew who he really was. And the man they'd thought him to be, another soldier he'd impersonated, was dead.

"She's going to know you're alive when the death benefits stop."

He'd thought of that. Had told his superiors that he didn't need to see a shrink, and the morning's meeting was only proving his point.

"I'll do whatever I have to do, sign whatever I have to sign, so that she continues to receive insurance coverage and monthly checks in the amount she expects." His salary should be able to cover that, with enough left for him to live on. They'd told him he'd have his pick of duties. After a mandatory six-month leave. And a release from the fly-voiced woman. All due respect to her, meeting with her was a waste of his time. She couldn't begin to see inside him. And wouldn't know how to handle it if she could. No amount of learning could prepare you…

"You indicated a desire to stay with the navy."

"Yes." It was all he had. He'd chosen his loyalty.

"Naval police," she said, glancing through the dark reading glasses sitting halfway down her nose at the open file on her desk. He'd considered going civilian…applying to the Naval Criminal Investigative Service, but then his checks to Emily would no longer come from the navy.

"Correct." Sitting back, his ankle across his knee, he reached an arm out along the back of the couch—a pose of relaxation he'd perfected over two years of living as family within an enemy sect. Pretending not to have a care in the world as he lied to them every single day, knowing that if he slipped up, was found out, he'd suffer torture far worse than death.

His free hand came to his chin and for a second, he was startled by the bareness there.

He'd shaved the beard. No longer had it to pull on when he needed to make certain he was still alive. And could feel.

He was Petty Officer First Class Winston Hannigan again. Not Private First Class Danny Garrison—the young man in his command who'd died in his arms, the man whose identity he'd assumed. If he'd died over there, as he'd expected to do, Danny would have been hailed as the hero. His family deserved that.

"You need my sign-off at the end of six months."

Hers, or another military shrink's. He looked her straight in the eye. After the past two years, Winston didn't scare easily. Was way beyond falling prey to intimidation or manipulation.

He'd lived with the enemy for two years and had come out with a body still fully intact. Not many visible scars, even.

"Tell me why you don't want your wife to know you're alive."

He'd already done so, when he'd first taken a seat in her office and she'd asked him to tell her a little about himself.

"I'm not the man she knew. Nor am I a man still interested in a lifetime commitment to another individual."

"So you said." The brunette fortysomething in dress whites kind of shrugged as she tried to pin him with her eagle eye. Wasn't going to happen. The only pins he wore were attached to his ribbons.

"It's not fair to her," he added, lest the woman think he'd developed a selfish streak during his time in pseudo-captivity. "I am not the man she married. She wouldn't love the man I've become. Trust me on this. I know her. She'd grieve every day, living with me. It's much kinder to let her make a new life for herself."

"She's not a woman who knows her own mind?"

"Of course she is. Completely. Emily knew when she was fourteen that she was going to be my wife. And she knew we had to have college degrees before we married, too," he said. "She's been with the same firm since graduation and has quickly climbed the ranks to senior account executive. Because she knows what she wants and goes after it."

"But you don't love her anymore."

"I didn't say that."

"Not exactly."

"Let's just say…my feelings have changed. Period. Across the board. I don't *love* anything in the ways I used to. For God's sake, I lived in hell for two years. I'm affected by that, okay? But not in any way that will prevent me from being a damned good MA." Master-at-arms—naval military police. The one thing he knew for certain he'd be good at.

"Of course you're affected. That's why you're here."

If his hour were up, he'd be leaving. But it wasn't. So he sat. Appeared relaxed. Thought about pulling on his beard. He knew the drill. Had lived it every day for the past twenty-four months. He was there because he had to be. No less. No more.

Five minutes of silence passed. Six. Then seven. Relaxing became more real than act. Silence was a friend he trusted. Within the silence he could hear.

Think. Prepare. Protect.

Within the silence he could be whoever he wanted to be. Think whatever he wanted to think.

"Here's what I believe." Dr. Adamson ruined the moment. "I believe that your six-month sabbatical was ordered to give you time to heal. And since we both know that, physically, you could pass any test today, your superiors must believe you need time to heal mentally. Or emotionally. Or, more likely, both."

"Could also be that having been in captivity for two years earned me six months of leave." Not that he was expecting the immediate future to be a vacation. He'd be debriefing with select, hand-chosen individuals. Two years of information collection was filed in his brain. No one asked him to collect it. But since he had, they wanted it. About as much as he wanted them to have it.

"The order isn't written as vacation leave time," she said, looking down as though rereading what she'd probably already committed to memory.

Semantics. He said nothing. Didn't move. Or drop his gaze from hers. Bring it on. Whatever she had to dish out...he could take. And then some.

"Your superiors think you need my help," Dr. Adamson said, closing his file and leaning her forearms on her desk over it as she looked at him. "In order to survive, you built defenses. Exactly what you've been trained to do."

He gave her a bit of a shrug. Probably of acknowledgment.

"Your task now is to let some of them go. That takes time. You know what you know. I'm not debating that. Or even saying it's wrong. But if you're going to be of any further service to the United States, to the navy, you need to figure out which of those defenses no longer serve you and lose them."

Right. Fine. He probably didn't have to listen to every conversation in the next room anymore as a way of watching his back. Or sleep a few hours every day in the bunker he'd dug so that he could stay awake during the night when others thought he was asleep. He didn't need to watch his back quite so much now that there were others around who'd share the burden while he watched theirs. Maybe he didn't need to control every single thought he had.

He'd already reached these conclusions. Didn't need her telling him what he already knew. But he needed her signature, releasing him.

If she wanted him to spell things out, he would. But only if it came to that or no signature. His thoughts were the one thing no one had taken from him.

"What you do is your choice, of course. Always. But for me to be able to release you back to active duty, in any capacity, I'm going to need some specific things from you."

His arm dropped from the back of the couch as he leaned forward. Ready.

"I'm going to need to see you at least twice a month over the next six months."

He'd been prepared for twice weekly. He hid a smile as he mentally applauded her good judgment. "Done."

"When you return, two weeks from today, I'd like you to have a more permanent place to live."

He was fine in the barracks. But…he could easily afford an apartment, too. He nodded.

"And I need you to go see your wife. If you want someone to prepare her ahead of time, let her know that you're still alive, I can see to that."

Had she listened to anything he'd said? The muscles in his jaw tensing, Winston clamped his jaws together.

Took a long, slow breath. Reminded himself that he was an officer in the United States Navy.

"Whatever arrangements the two of you make are up to you, but you have to make them. With her. Or her lawyer."

Her lawyer? As in divorce?

He supposed, if he was going to be alive to Emily, divorce would come, but…

"Let me get this straight. Before I can go back to serving my country… I have to hurt my wife? Make her suffer more than she already has?"

"You have to learn how to interact with people in a more normal interpersonal way, Officer. Your wife has a mind of her own. You don't have the right to take her choices away from her. Or her suffering, if that's what's to come her way. It's also important that you be capable of handling life's emotional ups and downs rather than running from them, but first and foremost, you can't go through life, at least not navy life, thinking that you know best for everyone else."

She was staring straight at him and one clear fact hit so hard he almost physically cringed. The navy had given her a charge. She could only release him back to them if she could confidently assure them that, in her opinion, he could, and would, follow orders.

He was paying for his choice to act of his own accord. His choice to go rogue.

And that, he understood.

Wednesday. June 19. He left Dr. Adamson's office, after one hour to the minute, having agreed to her demands.

All of them.

Chapter Four

She'd had the home pregnancy test for a week. Had carried the box in her bag for the first couple of days, then moved it to the cupboard by the toilet in the master bath.

It wasn't that she didn't want to know. She just didn't want to get her hopes up, or dashed, with false readings. The doctor had said two weeks.

So there she was, in a short gray skirt and matching short jacket, with three-inch heels and a silk blouse, dressed for her noon business meeting in LA, sitting on a plastic chair in an examining room at the Elliott clinic, having just peed in a cup. She'd given blood the day before.

She'd deal with facts. She just couldn't tolerate any more doubt-induced head games. Either she was, or she wasn't. If she was…then…

Tears spurted up out of nowhere and she took a deep breath.

And if she wasn't, she'd try again.

If she couldn't ever get pregnant… If the problem had been her all along… If there'd been a problem other than timing or over-trying…

The door opened and a doctor she'd never met before walked in. She could have received the news over the phone. The protection of the sterile little brick-walled examination room, with a calm professional discussing options, had seemed more doable to her.

"Well?" she asked, before the woman could even introduce herself. Dr. Hamilton, her tag read. Did it mean something that a doctor and not a PA had come to see her?

"Is something wrong?" she blurted. "I was expecting the nurse, or…"

"Christine asked me to speak with you."

Heart thudding and dropping like lead weight in her stomach, she straightened her back. "Something's wrong."

"No." The blond-haired woman, in dark pants and a purple short-sleeved blouse, pulled a stool over to sit in front of Emily. Close. Too close. The doctor smiled.

"You're pregnant," she said. "Due March 14. Christine thought you might have some questions."

Pregnant? She was pregnant? As in… Winston's child was right there, in the room with them, inside her, growing into life?

"I'm going to have a baby?" She couldn't make out Dr. Hamilton's features clearly. Tears blurred her vision. Trying to brush them away with a shaking hand, she shook her head. Wanted to apologize. Was afraid if she spoke, sobs would erupt.

Oh, good God, she was pregnant? After all those years of trying. Of disappointment.

"This is what you wanted, isn't it?" The doctor's voice reached her as though from afar. Because Emily had been far away—in other doctors' offices, in another room in that very clinic, with Winston, needing their baby so badly...

"Oh, yes!" she said, sniffling. Kind of giggling. "Yes, God, yes! I just... I guess I didn't really believe it would happen! I'm actually pregnant!" She grinned. Sniffled again.

Dr. Hamilton grinned back at her. "You'll have appointments to schedule, and we'll be prescribing vitamins and tests along the way, but for now, all you have to do is celebrate."

And buy a nursery. Call her mother. And Winston's parents. Or...

Maybe not yet. The nursery, okay. But the parents?

Lord knew she didn't want them descending on her. And they would. All the way from Florida—and most certainly from San Diego.

Besides, what if she...

"Am I at more risk for miscarriage? Since I was inseminated? And struggled to get pregnant to begin with?" She stared, solemn-faced, at the friendly doctor. Who was already shaking her head.

"The first three months are your highest risk, of course. But there's no indication in your history to lead me to think that this will be anything but a normal pregnancy. We'll do an ultrasound at sixteen weeks, or sooner, if you'd rather, just for your own peace of mind, but truly, the best thing you can do right now for you and your baby is to just be happy. Don't worry. Eat healthy, no alcohol or smoking, of course, and otherwise live your life as you normally would."

She nodded. She could do that. "Thank you," she said, grinning—and crying again, too. She was guessing it was too soon to blame that on hormones.

"Of course," Dr. Hamilton said. "If you have your own obstetrician, you'll need to schedule an appointment, but if you'd like us to continue to follow you, we'll get you scheduled for everything now."

They both stood, Emily on weak knees. "I'm staying here," she said. There'd never been any question on that one.

Dr. Hamilton opened the door, led the way down the hall, and for a second there, as she followed the woman, Emily hugged herself.

Wednesday, June 26. Winston's baby was growing inside her!

She prayed that wherever he was, he knew. And was smiling, too.

He'd been by the house twice. Once when he'd first arrived in San Diego. He'd rented a car and driven up to Marie Cove just to see the home he and Emily had purchased together. To see if he could tell if she was still living there.

The curtains had been the same—which didn't say a lot. The yard had been manicured in a way that pleased him—which was saying a lot, but not that she was still living there. He hadn't hung around long enough to notice anything else. Where she was hadn't mattered. What mattered was knowing she was okay.

He'd requested that someone he trusted on base ask around for him. And had toasted her with a few beers when he'd heard that she was still at the same firm, with the same home address. He knew nothing more than that. Hadn't wanted to know.

If she was remarried, living with someone, it was none of his business. He wished her well from the bottom of his heart. Needed her to be happy.

The second time he drove by, he'd meant to stop. In light of the agreement he'd made with the naval psychiatrist, he'd asked if he could be the one to let his wife know he was still alive. After all, he wasn't assuming a new identity. Which meant that they had to divorce for her to be free to continue living her new life. No one but him was going to be able to convince her of that. And her seeing what he'd become, understanding from the moment she heard he was still living that her husband was never coming back, was mandatory for her well-being.

But that Wednesday in June, a week after his first meeting with his shrink, he drove a different rental car right by the house he now knew to still be Emily's home, without even slowing down. Thing was, it struck him, turning onto that street, that the house was still his, too. His name was on the title.

Which made things messy. He didn't do messy these days. His life had one dimension left, and messy didn't compute there.

So he drove on by.

There were just too many cribs in the world. And not enough to choose from in the stores. Pulling into her driveway Saturday, just before noon, Emily barely noticed the car parked out front. Her mind was on the four-in-one convertible crib she'd seen online—the one with the drawer underneath and the far side that was taller than the others, like a headboard. She'd hoped to find it that morning, to have a chance to make sure in person that it was easy enough for her to manipulate alone before she purchased it. And she wanted it in white. Or brown. Half of what she'd seen was gray. As popular as the color was apparently becoming in the home design world, she just couldn't bring more gray into her life. And most particularly not into the nursery.

It wasn't until she'd pulled into her garage, pushed the button to close the door behind her, entered in through the kitchen and heard a knock on her front door that she thought of the car out front. A dark, expensive-looking sedan. In the back of her mind she'd figured it belonged to someone visiting the family across the street. The Bloomingtons had a lot of extended family, and an endless number of weekend get-togethers. They had a lovely backyard pool. Had invited her over a few times...

Reaching for the front door handle, she wondered if the visit was just that—another Bloomington family invitation. It was June, soon to be July. Warm and sunny. Made sense they'd be having a pool party...

Stopping just short of unlocking the door, she peered out the peephole.

What?

She knew the white dress uniform of the naval officer, thought maybe she recognized the female chaplain who accompanied him. And maybe the other guy looked familiar, too, a medical something or other. The team that had come within a day of Winston going missing two years before had looked eerily similar.

With a sick feeling, she stood still for a moment. Even with a mental rundown of every loved one she could ever remember having, she couldn't come up with someone they'd be there to tell her about. She'd already lost the only navy officer she'd ever loved.

Were they there about the baby? Winston's heir? No. She shook her head. That made no sense. But thinking of the small life inside her gave her the strength to straighten up and open the door.

"I'm Senior Chief Petty Officer Greg Hall…" The man introduced himself and the chaplain and medic with him. She stood frozen. "May we come in?"

Standing back, she let them enter, closed the door, showed them to the couch in the living room. Two years before, she'd brought them to the dining room table. And had had trouble eating at the table for weeks after they'd left.

She didn't use the living room much anymore. She was always in her office, where she had a comfortable lounger and television, or going to bed, when she was at home.

That would change, though. Now that she was going to be a family.

And then it hit her.

"I already got the letter," she said, before Officer Hall could do more than settle on the edge of the chair across from them. "I know Winston's been proclaimed dead."

"That's what we need to speak with you about, Mrs. Hannigan." Officer Hall, a man looking to be close to forty with a hint of silver at his temples, spoke as his small team watched her.

They were ready to react, she supposed, to needs she might express. Whether emotional or physical. Nice of them, really. But quite unnecessary at this point.

She'd held it together the last time a team had visited her, too. Back then she'd been certain that Winston would return to her.

"That letter… I don't quite know how to express this… it's unusual, to be sure…"

She waited. Felt for the guy. What, her death benefits weren't going to be as described? She could tell him she didn't care, but knew that the navy had its protocols. That there was probably a manual description Officer Hall was attempting to adhere to. Protocols were there for good reason, Winston always used to tell her.

Chaplain Blaine, her tag read on the navy blue jacket, leaned forward, almost reaching out a hand that, instead, landed on her own knee.

Hall coughed. "Are you here alone, ma'am?"

"Yes." If you didn't count the baby.

"And, since your husband was declared dead, are you in a relationship…?" He cleared his throat. "Is there anyone else who could or should be here with you?"

Frowning, Emily looked from one to the other of the three of them. All in their uniforms. Looking so…uncomfortable. She didn't get it. She'd already been told Winston was dead.

What could they tell her that would be worse than death?

"I don't need anyone here with me," she said. "I live alone. And no, I'm not in a relationship, though what that has to do with anything…" She let her words trail off as she heard the defensiveness in her tone. They were good people doing their jobs. Apparently a very difficult one that morning.

Stomach churning, Emily was taking a breath to ask what was going on when Officer Hall spoke.

"We're here to tell you that your husband is not dead, Mrs. Hannigan…"

He said more. She could hear the drone of a male

voice. Felt eyes on her. Met the gaze of the redheaded chaplain and locked there.

Your husband is not dead, Mrs. Hannigan.

Was she going crazy? Had he really said those incredible, beautiful, miraculous words? But…

There was compassion in the chaplain's gaze. Along with other things she couldn't decipher at the moment. But one thing was pretty clear. There was no light of joy. No sparkle. With jerky movements, she turned her head, taking in the two officers on either side of Chaplain Blaine.

"Winston's alive?" Before she could figure this out, she had to make certain she'd heard right. That she wasn't losing her mind right there in her own living room just three days after she'd found happiness again—in the form of the life inside her.

"Yes." Officer Hall nodded, as though to emphasize the word. Maybe knowing that emphasis was needed on her side of the room?

"He's alive!" She stood, clasped her hands, teared up, as all three officers remained seated, watching her. Seemingly concerned, as opposed to just being polite.

So though she needed to run outside and scream to the world, she figured that could wait until she was alone. She sat. Faced them.

"What's wrong?" It didn't matter what they told her. Her man was alive. They could get through anything else.

Winston was alive! And she had a baby to give him! There could be no mistake in that timing. Finally! Yes! Life was making sense again and…

"He's been living with extremists for the past two years, Emily," the chaplain spoke now. "He's not the man you knew him to be."

They had no idea what she knew of Winston—bodies changed, thoughts changed, even hearts changed sometimes, but souls…they were forever. And that's what she knew. Souls didn't change.

Winston had shared his with her. She still kept it tightly held within her heart.

"I realize that combat takes its toll," she said now. Had he lost his legs? Or maybe his face had been blown up? Whatever, she didn't care—other than for the pain he'd suffered and could still be suffering. "It's fine. I'm fully capable of handling it. Just tell me where he is and when I can see him."

"That's just it, ma'am," Hall said. "He doesn't want to see you. Not yet."

So he was that bad. She shook her head. Confused. Winston knew that while she was wildly attracted to him, physical appearance was only a small part of the bond between them.

"Not yet." She homed in on what she felt she could master in the moment. "When, then?"

"Soon," Chaplain Hall said while the medic remained alert, but mute. "He's going to contact you, but felt that just dropping in on you would be too much…"

Too much? Frowning, she was done with the polite talk.

"Tell me what's going on. What happened to him? He's capable of just dropping in? Where is he? And how long have you known he's alive?"

"We aren't at liberty to answer all of that," Hall said, his hat in his hands, literally. "I can assure you that physically, your husband is fine. In top shape. Mentally he's as sharp as ever."

Which left… "And emotionally?"

"He's a changed man, Mrs. Hannigan. You need to be prepared."

Suddenly she didn't want to hear any more. Not from a team. Not from strangers. "Do his parents know?"

"No. He's only been back in the States a short time. Because he was already declared dead, and because he's of sound mind, and because everything about him right now, everything he's been through, everything he knows, is of a sensitive nature, his wishes to remain as though dead were granted for a short time."

"So now they're being told as well?"

"Not yet. But soon."

"So I'm to keep quiet about this?" Finally, a charge she could grasp hold of. Something she could be a part of.

"That's up to you, Emily." Chaplain Blaine spoke again. "Winston made it clear that if you needed to talk with your parents, or his, you were to be at liberty to do so. We'd only ask that you give the navy a chance to visit them first."

She shook her head. Her husband obviously hadn't wanted their families to know yet. He'd have reasons. "I'm fine to wait," she said. "For as long as he needs."

Forever, if that's what it took him to be able to find his way back to her.

Because he would. She knew he would.

And when he did, she'd have a gift that would heal his hurting heart as only a miracle could do.

Chapter Five

He'd had no plan. Why hadn't he seen it? He'd changed his mind, told them to tell her and then he'd had no immediate plan for what came next. Shaking his head, Winston tried not to notice the possible mirrored shaking in his hand on the wheel of yet another rental car on Sunday morning.

He could buy his own car.

On base, he didn't really need one. Had been able to borrow a ride, or, for the trips to Marie Cove, rent a vehicle quite easily. Much cleaner. No loan. No mess. California was a "community property" state. If he bought something while married, his wife had joint ownership. And joint responsibility for any debt.

He had no right to land Emily with debt.

Renting a car, driving to Marie Cove, had been nowhere on Sunday's agenda. He'd had a visit from Officer Hall on Saturday afternoon, letting him know that

Emily was aware he was alive. And that she'd said she'd keep his being alive a secret until he wanted it otherwise.

That was it. Hall had given him nothing else. Not a word about how she looked. How she took the news. If she had another man in her life.

Not one damned thing.

How could he know how to proceed with her on nothing? He needed intel, for Chrissake. He'd worked out on the lifting machine. Then run. Had a late dinner. Tried to write a bit—doing as ordered and making notes of his time in Afghanistan, cataloging things that had happened as they came to him.

Eventually he'd slept—without the help of the sleep aid one of the doctors he'd seen over the past weeks had prescribed to him.

And woken to stare at the ceiling and wonder if Emily was doing the same. Staring at the ceiling. Trying to understand why the man who'd known her deepest fears—and her greatest desires and secret fantasies—didn't want to see her.

Had she asked how he was? Where he was?

What must her mind be doing to her this day? He'd been at the car rental place before they opened, and was on the road before he'd had time to think about the plan. And realized there wasn't one.

Was he just going to show up on the doorstep? Would it be kinder to call first? And how would that go? "Emily, this is Winston…"

She'd know his voice the second she heard it. Maybe. Unless tonal quality changed with loss of soul.

She wouldn't know the number. The navy had given him a temporary phone, pay-as-you-go, with its own number. Had Emily kept his number active? Been paying for it on their plan for two years even though he hadn't been using it?

He knew she had. It's what she'd do. Emily hadn't changed. He had.

Of course, she'd thought him dead. For at least a month. A billing cycle. The number might be gone.

He didn't think so.

Didn't know why he was obsessing over a frickin' number.

He wasn't going to call her. What would be the point? He had to see her. To work out the legal details. He'd given his word.

And now that she knew he was alive, she deserved the truth. She needed to know that he was dead inside. It was the only way to set her free.

Pulling into the drive, he took a deep breath, allowing himself to experience fully as he'd been ordered. And felt...nothing. He knew the slope. Most of the cracks. Saw the little dent in the garage, lower right, where he'd run the riding mower a little too close because he'd been busy gazing at his wife, who'd come outside in a pair of really short denim shorts and a black halter top.

His brain computed the memory. Nothing else happened. Not anywhere. Not even a little twinge beneath the fly of his uniform khakis.

He hadn't needed to wear them. He was off duty. He just needed to hit a store and get some clothes. Everything he'd had with him had been lost in the desert when he'd walked into the enemy camp and offered to become a traitor to his country to distract them long enough for his comrades to get to safety. Everything he'd left behind that day had been returned in a box of effects to his widow.

The navy had helped him get a new driver's license.

Had provided uniforms, skivvies, socks, shoes. Enough to last a few days. His barracks had a laundry facility.

He had to get out of the car to get the job done. So he did. Shut the door like a man with a job to do. Walked with straight shoulders and purpose toward the front steps. Climbed them.

The front door had been painted. It was beige now. Used to be white. Hand raised to knock, he was startled as the door flew open.

"Winston? Oh my God, Winston! I knew you'd come. I was waiting. I knew!" The chatter went on, slightly garbled with tears, as weight slammed against his body.

He grabbed for it, lest it fall. Or lest he did. Arms clung to him, around his neck, as breasts fitted against his chest in a familiar, completely natural way. His arms lowered enough to find their place at the curve of waist just below his waist as his foot scooted, allowing room for the smaller foot sliding in between his two.

The drill was embedded. As much of his naval training had been. It all came back to him with ease. Until Emily lifted her head, gazed into his eyes, and planted her mouth against his.

Lips pursed tightly closed, he stood there, eyes open.

And waited for her to figure out that the man she'd known and loved no longer existed.

Eyes closed, Emily couldn't have stood alone. Couldn't think at all. Her heart pounded with Winston's pulse, her hands clung to the warmth of the skin at his neck, her body leaning into him as it had always done.

Tears poured out of her, two years of sorrow, and joy, too, so much that she was wrapped in a sense of unreality—as though sensation was all there was.

No time. No place.

If heaven existed on earth, she was in it. And content to explode joy within it forever and ever. World without end.

Her lips on his were only more of the joining—not a kiss; basic lust was far too coarse for that world—as Winston seemed to know. He didn't open his mouth. Or devour her.

Even his usual hot and heavy desire respected their space. Souls long parted, together again. Nothing touched that.

At some point he picked her up and carried her inside. Snuggled up against his big strong navy man body, she held on, feeling uncharacteristically needy. Winston was home. She didn't have to be strong. To carry all the weight. She sniffled. Knew she had to stop the tears. They'd been bottled up for so long...

He laid her back against the couch. Let her go.

She waited for him to sit so she could climb up onto his lap. He'd liked it, when they'd go out to a bar, when she sat on his lap. She knew why.

Sex wasn't why she wanted to be there now. Their sexual connection could wait. She just needed the reality of him. The warmth. The feel of him breathing.

He didn't sit. At least, not on the couch. He lowered himself to the edge of a chair neither of them had ever used—not in her memory. It had come with the set. But he sat there now.

"You look good." She would remember those words forever. The first time she'd heard his voice in more than two years.

"I look a mess," she told him, suddenly conscious of the cutoff sweat shorts and T-shirt she was wearing, both his, while she'd been sitting at her computer, drinking decaffeinated tea and looking at cribs. Her hair was just hanging there. Long and…straight. She'd always curled it. Done fancy things with clips and scrunchies. He'd liked it because he'd loved undoing all her hard work.

If there'd been any makeup, which there hadn't, she'd have cried it all off anyway.

"You look good," he said again. His gaze hadn't left her. But for the first time in their lives, she couldn't be sure what was going on with him. He didn't seem to share her joy. Or seem…anything. Happy. Uncomfortable. Sad.

He's a changed man, Mrs. Hannigan. Officer Hall's words came back to her.

And she straightened up. Wiped her eyes. Took the handkerchief Winston handed her and cleaned up her face.

What a selfish witch she was being. Winston was the one who'd suffered. He needed her to be strong.

Just the day before, she'd sworn she'd handle whatever was to come, give him whatever he needed from her, love him back to health. She had it in her. There was no doubt about that.

Yet here she was falling apart like a sappy idiot. It was just that… With a small, intimate smile and fresh tears, she said, "You look good," right back to him.

Relief filled her when he nodded, seemingly pleased. And, oh God, he looked good. So good. Better than she'd ever imagined.

He'd been well fed—though he was as lean as ever. His skin tone was tanned and healthy. She didn't notice any scars, not that his uniform gave her a lot of opportunity in that area. His hair, as dark as always, was cut in its usual short style with the little bit of bang that she liked to run her fingers through just to tease him. His brown eyes were as big as she remembered, and those lips… still full of every ability to twist her stomach in knots.

"You're well?" he asked.

She grinned again. "I am now. It's been a bit lonely around here…"

His nod was curt, yet seemingly expressing satisfaction at the same time. She couldn't explain it, but accepted the thought just the same.

"And you?" she asked. Reading Winston had always been easy for her. Not so now, and yet it was more critical than ever. She didn't doubt for a second that she could do it if he gave her just a little more time. He was worth the effort.

"I'm well," he told her. Still watching her. She wasn't sure he'd even stopped long enough to blink. The stare might have been unnerving, except that this was Winston. Her soul mate, lover and best friend. Home again.

"There are things we need to discuss," he said.

She nodded. And then, in a flurry of realizations, jumped up and ran to a drawer in the kitchen. Pulling out the key ring, she started to cry again for a second. She'd thought those keys had been put permanently to rest.

"Here," she said, back in the living room, handing the keys to Winston. He took them, looked at them for a long few seconds.

Almost as though he didn't recognize them. Hall had assured her that his mental faculties were all there.

"Your car's still in the garage," she told him. His house keys were on that ring, too.

Oh my God! He's home!

His pillow won't be empty tonight! She had to make meat loaf for dinner. He particularly loved her meat loaf.

There was no ground beef in the house. She'd need to run to the grocery. Didn't want to leave him for even a second. So maybe they could go together. He might need a new toothbrush. His had been sitting unused in the cup for a long time. Did bristles get brittle?

"Your clothes are all still in your closet and drawers." She hurried into speech when he looked up at her with an expression she didn't recognize. "You can change if you like."

Yeah. Let him get comfortable. Thinking about his favorite shorts and T-shirts, remembering how he'd wear them on Sunday mornings because he could just relax, she was so thankful she'd held on to his things, rather than donating them as had been suggested to her by more than one well-meaning person. Her mother among them.

"Change?" He frowned.

"Into something more comfortable," she told him. "I'm assuming all the navy has provided you with is uniforms." Why else would he be in one so early on a Sunday morning?

He nodded. Frowned. And then nodded again, before he stood. "You mind if I go…" He pointed to the hall that led back to their bedroom.

"Of course not, Win, this is your home as much as it is mine!"

His hesitancy broke her heart, and she choked back the tears as she watched him. He seemed so hesitant. Unsure. Almost like he didn't belong in his own home.

As though he thought he had no rights.

This had to be what Hall had meant when he'd said Winston was a changed man. She could only imagine what had happened to him to strip him of his confidence.

A shard of anxiety curled through her, and she shook it away. He needed her strong. Capable.

But…what had they done to him?

Watching his straight back as he walked down the hall, wanting to follow him and sensing that she had to let him make the journey on his own, she couldn't help noticing that he looked neither right nor left, didn't glance into their office, the spare bedroom or bath, went right past the wedding photos on the wall as though they weren't there…

Whatever had happened, she didn't have to know right now. In his own time, he'd tell her. For now, her job was to love him. To help him find his way back. To show him the way, if she had to. To let him know that whatever had been done to him, whatever, didn't change him and her, fighting their way through life together. Didn't change them.

He'd been given back to her. That was all that mattered.

Their love would do the rest.

Chapter Six

How could he have walked into this without a plan? Everything was about the plan. Without a plan, there was chaos.

Chaos was unacceptable.

Walking to the back of the house, Winston worked his mind toward a plan. For that, he needed a goal. He had two. Active duty. That was clear.

And Emily's well-being. No more pain for her. She needed to be free of him.

Very clear.

And not so clear at all.

In her bedroom, he stopped, half concerned that she'd follow him. He had no plan for that, either. But knew he didn't want it to happen.

When he was certain he was still alone—there was no movement of air that indicated otherwise—he took a quick glance around.

Nothing about the space had changed. The wedding ring he'd dropped on the nightstand on the side of the bed he'd used to sleep on—a ritual any time he left on assignment, their symbol that he'd be back—was still right where he'd dropped it, in a small circle thick with dust. For more than two years, she'd dusted around it. She'd never picked it up.

That was to have been his job. His promise that he would be back. That she wouldn't get the ring back from a uniformed official. Or hear that it had been lost with him at sea.

So here was a fact. Emily was still living in their past. He had to free her of him so she could move on and be well. Happy.

Just leaving her alone, living somewhere else, wasn't going to do that. Two years of living as the husband of another woman in an Afghan desert hadn't done it—holing up in the barracks in San Diego certainly wasn't going to. Not that she knew about poor Afsoon—the woman who'd been made to marry him sight unseen who had shed tears when she'd had to share his bed.

But even if he told Emily about Afsoon, he knew what she'd say—the same thing his superiors all said. He'd done what he had to do to save lives.

They were all right.

But finding out that he was capable of… He shook his head. Coming back served no purpose. He knew what he knew. About himself. About life.

And didn't believe in any of the things Emily's house proclaimed. The love she'd thought she'd been keeping alive didn't exist. Not in the form they'd always thought. Hard to fathom how he could ever have believed it did.

They'd been kids, pure and simple. Naive.

He'd made promises he hadn't kept. Taken vows he could no longer honor. He had to be accountable for that. Had to set her free. It was all about her freedom. Yes. He could do whatever it took for the freedom of others.

And sometimes plans were fluid. They had to be. Spur of the moment, even, based on what the enemy put before you. The unseen and sometimes unknown.

You simply had to assess the hurdles. Which was him. Yes, he was the hurdle to Emily's freedom. To her eventual happiness. A happiness based on truth, not the lies of youth.

So that was it. He had to dispel the lies. Show her the truth. Not by leaving her. He couldn't stand in that room and not be aware of the damage his simply walking away would cause.

No, he had to show her. In as kind a way as possible. Minimize the pain.

The plan was forming.

Life was about doing what you had to do until you died.

And if you were a decent man, you did your duty.

She gave him ten minutes. When there was no movement coming from the bedroom in all that time, Emily trusted her gut and went to find Winston. To help him. She had no idea how hard this had to be for him. Couldn't hope to put herself in his shoes.

But when he hurt, she hurt. Pure and simple.

She had something that would bring him great joy. She had the healing tonic, growing right inside her. And all of the love and patience he could ever need to help him get to it.

He didn't seem to have moved since entering the room.

Still in full uniform, not a drawer opened or a closet door, not even a button undone, he stood there, staring at his nightstand.

The ring.

How could she have forgotten about the ring?

Having lived around it, moved around it, for so long, it had almost become a part of the furniture.

A revered one, but still...

The deal was that he'd retrieve it when he got back. Moving quietly, but quickly, she snapped the ring off the nightstand. Dusted it with the hem of her shirt. Grabbed Winston's left hand and slid the ring in place.

It still fit.

That mattered.

"Deals change," she told him, meeting his gaze as he looked down at her. "The love doesn't."

He said nothing. Took his hand from hers. But didn't remove the ring.

They faced each other. She wasn't intimidated. Like always, she had his back. He'd been through hell to get home to them. It was her turn to do their work. Or something like that.

"I understand that things change, Win. That things happened while you were gone, with both of us. I also know that our love is stronger than anything that life can dish out. No matter what happened. Or what changed. I'm here. You have my total support. And I'm absolutely thrilled, beyond anything I'll ever be able to express, that you're home. You, the man you are now. Welcome home."

His lower lip jutted, giving his chin a small pucker.

"So, what do you want to do first?"

"I have to return the rental car by five."

Innocuous words. They felt huge. "Okay, I'll follow

you. I'm assuming you rented it in San Diego?" It's where the base was.

Where her mother and brother were, too, but there was no way she was exposing Winston to family. Not until he was ready.

At the moment, she had no idea when that might be.

One second at a time.

That's how she'd dealt with his disappearance. His official death. And that's how she'd deal with life, too, for as long as it took.

"I didn't intend to stay here tonight."

She shook her head. The past two years had taught her a lot about her own strength. She could and would stand her ground on what mattered. "This is your home, Win. Where else would you stay?"

"The barracks."

"Why?"

He stared at her—it wasn't normal, those looks. There was nothing for her to read in his eyes.

He's changed. Emotionally.

Chaplain Blaine had left her card. Emily would call her as soon as she could. The chaplain and the others had assured her that Winston was not a danger to himself or others. To the contrary, he'd been open and honest about all that was going on with him. They'd needed her to understand that life's experiences changed people.

"I said I didn't *intend* to stay here tonight—that wasn't my plan when I first appeared at the door. I have since come to the conclusion that it would be best if I did. Stay, that is. With your permission. However, if my being here makes you uncomfortable, in any way, I am fine to drive myself back to San Diego and stay in the barracks."

Hands on her hips, she stepped closer to him. "Let's

get one thing clear, Winston Dane Hannigan. You are my husband. For better or worse. Until I no longer have breath in my body. This is *our* home, not just mine. You own it equally, and are equally responsible for it. I kept it running for us. I now expect you to take over your part. If, however, you don't want to be around me, then we'll work out a way to coexist here until you do."

Her heart should be shattering. It just wasn't. Winston was home! He was damaged, and that hurt…badly. But this wasn't about her. Love…it truly meant fighting the other's fight. And he had one hell of a big one in front of him. She was on it. Full force.

He could leave. She wouldn't stop him. Neither would she make it easy for him.

"I think it would be best if you followed me to San Diego. I'll return the rental car and, if you have time, I would like to stop by the barracks and get the few things I've accumulated over the past two weeks…"

Two weeks.

"Did you say two weeks?" she asked. Officer Hall had said he'd been back a "short time." She'd assumed days.

"I crawled out of the desert a little over two weeks ago, yes."

"How little?" He must think her nuts, standing there grilling him like the exact moment mattered.

But it did. Had she been inseminated with his sperm the same day he'd officially made it back to them?

"It was a Wednesday. A little over two weeks ago."

The exact same day.

It was a sign. Had to be. She just had to hold on. To serve him as he'd served his country. Life was happening as it was meant to. Winston was going to need a miracle to heal. And the very day he'd escaped, she'd taken the step to create his miracle.

He continued to assess her. She wanted to tell him. Was bursting with their news. But something told her to keep her counsel for the moment. At least until she got him officially out of San Diego.

And had a chance to speak with the chaplain, or whoever else she might refer.

"You want to change before we go?" she asked him. "You used to hate being in uniform on Sundays at home."

He didn't even glance toward his side of the closet before he shook his head.

"Let's go then." She couldn't get this chore done fast enough. She needed him moved back in, even if that only meant a couple of sacks in the back of her car.

Or his. An idea occurred to her. "Let's take your car," she told him. "I've been taking it out regularly, keeping it serviced. And since you'll be driving us back..."

He loved his car—an old Camaro he'd restored while they were in college.

He might have hesitated, but she couldn't be sure. She was busy leading the way. Out of their bedroom and down the hall.

"Emily."

Her name on his lips. In his voice. Lovely chills ran through her. She turned.

"If there's anything you want or need to know, anytime— if you ask, I'll answer honestly. If I can."

If I can. There could be military implications there. Things he wasn't at liberty to say. Or maybe he was telling her there were things he couldn't bring himself to talk about.

Either way, she had a feeling what he needed from her most, whether he'd admit it or not, was her patience.

"And that goes both ways," she told him. "Anything you ask, I'll answer honestly." It got quiet between them. Not awkwardly, just like it mattered. Like they'd somehow just repeated vows they'd taken years before. When they'd promised never to lie to each other. She'd never doubted that those vows still lived.

Obviously, he had.

Not sure what to make of that, Emily filed the moment away. She had a feeling that that mental file drawer was going to be growing in the coming days.

And even that knowledge didn't steal her joy.

Winston was home!

Chapter Seven

Winston almost took Emily up on her offer to drive the rental, leaving the Camaro for him. The sight of the Glacier Blue beauty with the dark blue interior had him gravitating toward it. Just to take a look. He'd put way too much time and money into the machine. Had given importance to it that hadn't mattered.

At least he'd done a good job.

"You sure you don't want to drive it?" Emily, in tight white capris, a loose black tank and a pair of black jeweled flip-flops, asked. She had her own set of keys in her hand. He'd pocketed the ones she'd given him.

"You're not listed on the rental contract," he said, and climbed behind the wheel of the nondescript four-door sedan.

Duty was what mattered. Serving his country. Breaking the law, even a rental contract law, was not in the plan.

The plan.

It was taking a major detour. But at least it was there. Telling Emily that they weren't going to work, that her only way to happiness was apart from him, even that he'd betrayed her, wasn't going to help him reach the goal. Two seconds in her presence and he'd known that. Like his superiors, she'd forgive him anything, put it down to the untenable situation, see the hero in him. She still believed.

The only way to get the truth through to her was to show it to her, directly and unflinchingly, day by day. There'd be painful moments, but they'd fade in time. When she was away and free and living with the happiness she deserved.

His focus had to be on keeping the end in mind.

He led the way to San Diego, watching his rearview mirror and adjusting his speed and turns as needed to allow Emily to stay behind him. And after he dropped off the car, he told her she could drive the short distance from the rental office to the barracks, then he got in on the passenger side, handing her his ID to show at the gate.

So, yeah, the car smelled…good. Familiar. His body recognized the seat's contour. He could almost feel the leather steering wheel cover beneath his grip. He turned the old but shiny crank to lower the window. Felt the power beneath him as Emily pulled into traffic.

For a second, life felt good.

He was definitely going to keep the car.

As badly as Emily wanted to traipse right beside Winston to collect his things, she stayed with the car. She had to be able to let him out of her sight.

Needed to give him space.

She didn't need professionals to tell her either of those

things. She was getting cues from him. She'd always known him that well.

And he, her.

It was one of the things that had built such intrinsic trust between them from the very beginning—this ability to read the other. To just know. They'd been fourteen, freshmen in high school, when they'd run into each other rushing to get into the building and out of the rain. She'd just had a fight with her brother. Her irritating sibling had just turned sixteen and with his driver's license he'd also been given the responsibility for driving her to school. That day, he'd refused to drop her off on her side of the building because in those days he'd refused to do anything she'd asked. He'd ruled. Winston had been late because his mom and dad had had a fight and he'd stayed to referee.

They'd both been bothered by more than the rain. He'd made a joke about it. About rain being fitting for the morning. Knowing she'd agree. And then asked if she wanted to meet him at lunch to see if either of their days had gotten any better.

Such a small thing. But the beginning of the rest of her life. The best part of her life.

Sitting in the passenger side of his Camaro, awaiting his return, she acknowledged to herself that their current situation wasn't perfect. Or even remotely like anything she'd imagined during the two years of waiting for him to return to her. She hurt for him. Worried for him. And yet…her spirit soared. They could deal with whatever was to come. She had no doubts there. As long as they were together, they'd be fine.

And the baby! She burst with the need to tell him. And yet sensed that the time wasn't right. Obviously, whatever had happened to her beloved husband had affected him emotionally. He'd always been such a sensitive guy. As strong as they came. Able and willing to do whatever it took to get a job done. And yet…his heart had been huge. And wide open to her.

So they had work to do. The enemy had closed his heart's door. Her job was to help him open it. Yeah, maybe it was going to take a miracle.

She sat there alone in the car grinning like an idiot.

Because she was carrying that miracle.

Platitudes, "you got everything?" "yes," "you need to stop anywhere else?" "no," filled the first part of the drive as they left San Diego. Two years driving alone and yet Emily felt completely natural in the passenger seat while he drove the car that had been sitting without him for so long.

Surreal, sure. But right.

"I thought I'd make meat loaf for dinner," she said as they pulled onto the highway that would take them north toward home.

He nodded. Adjusted his seat. Turned the ancient radio on and then back off again.

She suggested a stop at a big-box store so he could get that toothbrush, anything else he needed, and she could get some ground beef. He was fine with that, named a store closer to Marie Cove so the meat wouldn't spoil. And then he was silent again.

So silent.

Shutting her out? Or just shut in?

"I thought I'd take the day off tomorrow," she offered another five minutes down the road. "We could drive down to the beach. Or hike the cliffs above the beach in town." It was more a walking path than anything, but they used to hang out up there, watch the ocean, solidify their future.

"I have meetings at the base all day tomorrow."

Glancing at him, she frowned. Did he really? "I thought you were on a six-month leave." Officer Hall had said something about that before he'd left the day before.

"I'm not on active duty, but I have duties. Information to convey."

Stifling the first flood of feeling that came up—resentment against the job that had already taken so much of him from her—she reminded herself that Winston loved the navy. He needed to serve.

And it was probably good for him to have a normal routine. Sitting around doing nothing had never been his way. And probably not good for someone who had two years' worth of bad memories to purge.

Settling back in her seat, her head against the rest, she spent the next half hour telling him about the accounts she was working on, about people who'd come and gone from the firm where she worked, giving him updates on those he'd known.

He didn't seem to mind.

What in the hell was he going to do about bedtime? With no intention of resuming married life with Emily, he couldn't just go climb into bed with her.

But if he didn't, she'd merely set to waiting for him to get better. Her patience could last a damned lifetime. Her lifetime.

He needed her to see the truth. The plan was to show it to her.

Life wasn't about the beach anymore. Or gazing at the

ocean and dreaming silly dreams. It was about keeping focus on the goal. In the end, that was all that lasted— the need for focus. For the decent guy to serve the goal.

She suggested stopping at the cell phone store to get him a new phone. She'd been paying for his line all along, still had the same number active. He went along with her, chose a new smartphone, because there was no good reason not to do so. And he needed one.

Over dinner, her sitting in her normal seat, him in his, eating off the same dishes they'd bought together, from the same cupboards they hadn't changed since they'd moved here, she gave him a rundown of their finances. She'd done an impressive job for them. Incredible, really. In two years' time, she'd almost doubled their wealth. Not that it made them wealthy. But they were definitely more comfortable than when he'd left.

Which meant she hadn't done much spending. Or much living.

"I recognize that outfit," he said, nodding toward her capris and shirt. "You wear that for my benefit, because it's something I'd recognize? And you know I like it?"

"Yes."

"Well, don't. Wear whatever you'd normally wear. I know you'll have clothes I haven't seen, that you'll know people I don't know." That life had changed for them both.

Though, looking at the house, he couldn't see much evidence of it for her. It was as though he'd just walked out the day before and come back in.

"This is what I'd normally wear," she said, her tone soft. Understanding.

When she didn't understand. At all.

It was as though she'd put her life on hold for him. All of it. Except work. Which put even more distance between them.

She'd held on so tightly. He hadn't held on at all.

What in the hell was he going to do about bed?

After dinner, he did the dishes. She hovered. In and out of the room. Wiping the table. And then bringing him over to look at the computer, showing him their accounts. Explaining decisions she'd made. Asking his opinion. They talked about a couple of options. Agreed upon them.

He looked over at his own computer, on the other side of the partner desk they'd purchased from an antiques dealer. Had no interest in starting up the machine. The updates would take forever.

She asked if he wanted to watch a movie. Started talking about a couple she'd seen that she figured he'd like. And told him about the streaming services she'd signed up for.

Something new. Different. Apart from him.

Good.

He didn't feel like a movie. He wanted to sleep. He'd been doing a lot of that in the couple of weeks he'd been back.

What in the hell was he going to do about bed?

"You go ahead," he told her, referring to the movie offer. "I would rather just turn in."

It was barely eight o'clock. They used to rarely go to bed before eleven. At least to sleep.

The stricken look that crossed her face made him feel bad. And also made him feel like he was doing the job he'd come to do, too. Showing her.

"I'm so sorry, Winston. I wasn't thinking... Of course

we'll go to bed. I, um, actually…have been going to bed earlier myself."

She sounded…odd…as though she felt uncomfortable about the admission. Because she'd changed up their routine? God, he hoped she didn't feel guilty about that.

"About your sleeping… Are you okay in our bed? Will it bother you to have me there beside you?"

What in the hell was he going to do about bed?

If he answered in the affirmative, she'd understand, be patient, wait for him to heal.

"No, it won't bother me," he said, standing there in the office they used to share, still in his uniform khakis. "But I completely understand if it bothers you," he added. "You've been alone a long time. I'm somewhat of a stranger to you. I have no problem taking the spare room."

Eyes wide, horror evident, she was in front of him in an instant, her face inches from his. "There's no way I want you anywhere but in bed with me, Winston. You have to know that. We'll get through this, just like we get through everything. Together. I'm truly just so thankful you're alive, still having a hard time believing you're really here, but there's no way you're a stranger to me."

He swallowed. Nodded. And turned to go to bed.

Hands shaking, Emily brushed her teeth and pulled on Winston's favorite filmy blue negligee. He might be emotionally clogged, but Officer Hall had said physically, her husband was just fine.

And one thing she knew for certain about Winston, he had a lusty sexual appetite. Even after all their years of marriage, he'd still been hungry five out of seven nights a week whenever he was home.

He'd been without for two years.

She knew what that meant. It would probably be quick for him.

She was mentally prepared for that. Didn't care if it was over in five seconds. She'd been without his touch, without the feel of him inside her, for two years, too. She'd gotten pregnant with his baby without him inside her. Even one second would be enough for her for now.

He'd been under the covers when she'd finished turning off her computer and locking up the house. He'd already checked the doors before they'd gone to the office, but she wanted to give him time on his own to reacclimate with his things. As far as she could tell, he still hadn't looked in his closet or any of his drawers.

"Would you like the television on?" she called from her sink in the master bath. They'd never slept with it on the past, but she'd heard about guys who'd come home from particularly hard tours who'd suddenly been unable to sleep without it.

They needed it to drown out memories that came in the dark of the night.

"No, but it won't bother me if you'd like to watch for a while."

Thinking that maybe the television would help him relax, she turned out the light, picked up the remote and, once she was beneath the covers, turned on the TV. Winston lay flat on his back. Eyes already closed.

After a minute, she turned off the television. Slid carefully down until her head was on her pillow. And lay there. His breathing was even. Too even. He didn't snore, but there'd been a depth to his breaths when he slept. She had to figure that hadn't changed, which meant he wasn't actually asleep.

Thinking of him, in physical need, lying there stiffly,

willing to sacrifice himself and not touch her as he gave her time to get used to having him home and sharing her bed again, she swallowed back tears. Putting his own needs last was exactly what Winston would do.

And she knew what she had to do. Exactly what she wanted so desperately to do.

Turning on her side, facing him, she scooted over. Not crowding him. But close to him. When he didn't turn away, she knew she was on the right path. Reaching out a hand, she touched his chest, surprised to come into contact with a T-shirt. Winston never slept with a shirt on.

But...okay. Someday she'd ask him why, what had happened to him to prompt him to need a shirt at night. Someday.

For those first few minutes she was just plain selfish. Reacquainting herself with the feel of his chest. T-shirt and all. The muscles, the breadth, it was all exactly as she remembered. He didn't move, but she hadn't really expected him to. His self-control was about as strong as everything else about him, and after two years, he'd be holding himself in check.

A memory surfaced. She'd been seventeen...and knowing she was going to have sex with Winston for the first time. He hadn't wanted their first time to be in a car, or on a night when he had to leave her. He'd insisted they wait until they could spend the whole night together.

She'd been so afraid of disappointing him. He, she'd later found out, had been worried about hurting her. She'd made the first move that night, too.

When the T-shirt became too much of a barrier, Emily slid her hand down to the hem and up underneath it, feeling his skin like an electric shock through her system.

The warmth, the hair that spread across his belly and up-ward...every sensation was homecoming to her.

Pure, blissful. Right.

As Winston lay still, silent, Emily grew bolder. And more blatant in her intentions. He'd taught her every single erogenous inch of his body and how to stimulate them, and she remembered it all. With a flick of her finger, she teased his nipples. The left always got him harder than the right, so she played with the right first. He liked a little tongue mixed in, too, but aware that he might not last long, she didn't want to come on too strong.

While he didn't touch her—probably trying to stay in control since she knew that touching her turned him on fast—she was getting revved up with every second that passed. It didn't take her long to know she was ready to host him, and she moved her hand slowly lower.

He used to sleep nude, but would lounge in a pair of loose cotton boxers, and considering the T-shirt, she figured he'd have them on, too, was already remembering how to maneuver the waistband by the time she reached it.

A quick glance told her that Winston still had his eyes closed. No matter. Silent sex was the most intimate some-times.

There were no words that could live up to this moment.

Holding her breath as mind-altering sensations swarmed through her, she moved her fingers beneath the elastic at Winston's waist and down. Moved her body, too, getting ready to move over him, to settle on top of him.

He'd push up and into her hand first, and then into her. It was a dance they'd perfected.

He didn't push up. But the change in their moves didn't

faze her. She was making love to her husband. He was letting her. Nothing else mattered.

With her breath almost catching on a sob, she slid her hand slowly downward, anticipating her first feel of him in two long years. The velvety hardness and...

He wasn't hard. At all.

Shaking, and cold now, too, Emily looked up at him. He turned over, giving her his T-shirted back. He'd never even opened his eyes.

Chapter Eight

Winston lay awake most of the night. It took stern discipline to remain still, his back to the woman he'd once thought of as the other half of himself, knowing that she was hurting. He couldn't tell if she was crying, but he was fairly certain that she was. The Emily he knew would have been. But to roll over and console her, would, in the long run, be cruel, knowing as he did that things weren't going to get better for them.

That any consolation she took from him would be a lie. He wasn't her soul mate. Their love wasn't real because love wasn't real.

Duty. Loyalty. Those were what truly mattered. They came with a price, but he believed in their existence. Stood for them.

She fell asleep at 12:03, almost four hours after her botched attempt at sex with him. He knew by the sound of her breathing. The way her hand fell to the bed between them, her fingers in contact with his back. As gently as he could, he leaned far enough away that if she awoke, she wouldn't find herself touching him.

Otherwise he didn't move at all. Not even when, shortly after five, she got up. Left the room. Presumably to make coffee. She'd pulled on a robe on the way out.

He'd give her long enough to get a cup of coffee in her hand and then go out to her. Ask her if she had any questions. Or wanted him to find another place to stay.

She'd say no. She wasn't going to let a little thing like a failed hard-on come between them. But he had to make the offer.

Just as he had to tell her anything else she wanted to know. Like why he couldn't have sex with her and never would again.

Even if she asked, even if she listened to his explanation, he knew the dream wouldn't die easily. He knew what she was in for in the coming weeks, because he'd already been through it. He'd clung, too, at first. Refusing to give up. To give in.

But when it had come to choosing either his dream or the lives of his countrymen, his dream or the ability to help protect Americans from terrorist threats, the dream hadn't had a chance.

Truth was, the dream was just that, a dream.

She'd get it. And if he could make it hurt less, he'd do that. She was a good person. A great human being. He respected her more than anyone he'd ever known.

In boxers with cars on them—the first pair he'd encountered in his drawer the night before—he made a stop at the master bath before heading out into the hall. Maybe he'd be wrong and the night before would have been enough for Emily. Maybe she'd be more ready than he thought to discuss legal disentanglement.

They could afford it more easily than he'd expected.

Two steps into the hall and he stopped. Stared at the closed bathroom door halfway between him and the living room. Because it sounded to him like Emily was puking her guts out.

Painfully, brutally regurgitating. Even when there didn't seem to be anything left in her stomach.

What the hell? She was ill? And she hadn't said anything?

Jackass, what chance did you give her? You, firmly focused on your plan, failed to factor in the unknown. You looked, saw she was buried in the life you'd left and assumed nothing else had changed.

Was it cancer? Wouldn't someone have told him if she was taking chemo?

Or...*jackass*, maybe she just had the flu.

Maybe he was making her sick. Maybe this was coming from the trauma of finding out he was alive, followed by him on her doorstep the next morning, and then finding out that he wasn't at all the man she'd thought she'd married.

If positions were reversed, and he'd still been believing in their fantasy, he'd probably have felt sick, too.

Reaching in the hall closet for a washcloth, he tapped on the door and opened it, taking in Emily's body, in the blue silk robe he'd bought her for an anniversary weekend at a luxury resort on the beach. She was pretty much hugging the toilet, her head resting on her arm. The sink was on, cloth beneath the flow within a second. And then he was on his knees, gently wiping.

She flushed the toilet without raising her head. Looked

up at him, seemed to be grateful and then had another bout of dry heaves.

Back and forth between her and the faucet he spent the next ten minutes cooling the cloth and wiping her forehead and face, her neck.

And then she was done. Sitting up. Standing. Apologizing.

"I put coffee on for you," she said, heading back out to the kitchen, where he found her picking up a cup with a tea bag hanging out of it. Tea? Since when did Emily start liking tea?

Morning coffee had been the only way either one of them had been capable of starting a day.

Though Afghanistan was steeped in tea tradition, he'd been lucky enough to have good coffee the entire time he was there. Still needed it to get going in the morning.

"Em…are you okay?" he asked, using his shortened version of her name without thinking.

"Yeah."

She wasn't meeting his gaze. Because of the failed sex or the puking, he wasn't sure.

"It didn't seem that way a few minutes ago."

"I'm fine."

"You're not sick? As in… Have you been diagnosed with something you aren't telling me about?"

"I'm as healthy as a horse. My most recent checkup was last Wednesday."

Relief flooded him. Like when he'd touched down in the US for the first time in over two years.

"So what was that?"

She shrugged.

"Has it ever happened before?" Maybe she'd changed more than he thought. Had developed a weak stomach.

Had it happened when he went missing? Had she developed her own form of PTSD? Was this it? Because of him?

"No," she said. And then, moving to the dining room table, pulled out a seat. "Sit down," she told him.

After pouring a cup of coffee, he did as she asked. He didn't have anywhere to be until midmorning, when he met with someone from the anti-terrorist group. The questions he could answer, or insights he could give on active situations, were his reason for being alive.

She was staring at him in a whole new way. More assessing than anything. He knew that was good. That his plan was already working, as he'd known it would. She was separating from him. Questioning what she believed them to be.

He met her gaze straight on.

"I'm pregnant, Winston. Only two weeks, which I'm pretty sure is too early for morning sickness, but I guess, with the shock of this weekend, on top of everything else, morning sickness came early. It's the only thing that makes sense. Plus, it was exactly what I read about. Came on suddenly, out of nowhere, and was gone just as quickly. Dr. Miller told me to keep a box of saltine crackers by the bed. I just didn't think I'd need them this soon…"

He heard her voice. Watched her lips move. Stared. Focused. And couldn't compute.

"Winston?"

She was frowning at him.

"Did you, um, say…you're *pregnant*? As in, having a baby?"

He didn't glance down at her belly. Couldn't. But…the day before she hadn't looked… She'd had on those tight white pants and…a loose top. Since he'd kept his eyes firmly shut when she'd climbed in the bed and gotten out of it that morning, he couldn't say if she'd looked…

"Two weeks," she said, calmly. Right. She might have mentioned. But she was sitting there telling him she was pregnant. Couldn't there at least be some kind of inflection in her voice?

Shouldn't there be?

Two weeks…

She was in a relationship with someone else and he'd just landed on her doorstep. Shouldn't she have said something?

But how could she? They were still legally married. And he'd just come from two years of captivity. She had no way of knowing he'd walked of his own accord into that enemy camp. Or that he lived like family while he was there.

But…two weeks pregnant and she'd tried to have sex with *him*?

Oh, hell. Surely she hadn't been thinking to pass the kid off as his? That would be a stretch considering that they'd been trying—and failing—to get pregnant before he'd joined the ground crew and been shipped off.

He couldn't count the number of times over the past year that he'd been thankful pregnancy hadn't happened. That he hadn't let down his child as well as his wife. That a child hadn't been fathered by a man who knew that the concept of love was a huge fallacy.

Kids needed the fantasy. The security of belief allowed by the emotion called love.

His mind processed. He stared, needing the silence. For whatever reason, Emily allowed the quiet. Maybe because she was waiting for him to figure out that they had one hell of a dilemma in front of them.

"Does he know about me? That I'm alive?"

She frowned. "Who?"

"The...father." The man who'd slept with Emily after him. Just as he'd slept with Afsoon. So maybe, when he had time to adjust to the change, he'd see that all was good. Emily was a lot closer to reaching the truth than he'd thought judging by her actions the day before.

Her hand on his should have been a warning, but he was a bit stupefied. It was early. He'd only had a couple of sips of coffee. And she'd dropped one hell of a bomb-shell on him.

"You're the father, Winston. I thought you'd understand that. You're the only man I've ever even wanted to be with."

"You thought I was dead." Did she think he blamed her for taking a lover? He'd meant no accusation at all in his words. Simple facts were all he was looking for. To fit into the plan.

His brain replayed her words a second time, with a bit more focus. Enough to get the gist.

Emily was losing it on him.

She thought she was pregnant. And thought he was the father?

"I can't be the father, Em. I wasn't even in California two weeks ago."

So maybe she wasn't pregnant after all. Maybe she was just falling apart. He couldn't blame her...but he should probably make a phone call. Get them some help.

"I used your sperm...you know, that we had stored at the lab? I've been paying to keep it there and when I heard that you were dead... I had myself inseminated. I..." She shook her head. "I thought… It's a miracle, Winston." She took his hand, laced her fingers through his. "I was honoring you, and us, by bringing a piece of you to life, continuing your legacy. And now, with you here, it's what we always wanted. The plan is finally coming to be…"

The *plan*? It took him a second to realize that she was referring to the cockamamy dream they'd had to get married, have four children and grow old together in Marie Cove.

Except that they hadn't been able to conceive. And they'd just started delving into fertility treatment options when he'd shipped out and never returned.

Oh God. He could feel himself pale.

She was pregnant? With his child?

She couldn't be! He hadn't realized he'd spoken aloud, with all of his horror evident in his voice, until she whitened, too. Dropping his hand, she stood.

"I have to get ready for work," she said, and headed back to the shower.

He watched her go. Knew he shouldn't follow her.

And didn't try to stop her, or even speak, when, half an hour later, she passed him on her way to the garage door, bag and keys in hand.

"I'll see you tonight," she said at the door. "I love you, Winston. Be safe."

And she was gone.

Chapter Nine

She didn't go to work. Not right away. How could she?

No one in town or at work knew that Winston was back. Or that she was pregnant. They'd figure out both soon enough. Winston sooner than the baby. He'd be seen in town. In the neighborhood.

She planned to tell her boss, Steve Adeleigh, about Winston that morning, of course, and some of the people she worked with, but she had to get in a better frame of mind first. She'd already decided to keep news of the baby to herself until she passed the first trimester. Just hadn't wanted the questions. Now, with Winston's return, people could just assume she'd conceived naturally.

She'd distanced herself from her friends, anyway, and she was grateful for that now—grateful not to have anyone around who could read her well enough to see that she wasn't herself. Couldn't add the tension of having her mom drive up from San Diego, or Winston's parents fly in. Not until they'd had a little bit of time to adjust.

To figure out what they were going to look like in this new together.

She drove for half an hour. By the house a few times. Wanting to be in there with him. To know where he'd be.

To be sure he'd be there when she got home. That he'd be sleeping in their bed that night. Or at least in their house.

To know that he was okay.

To help him. Hold him. Let her love seep back into him.

Starting to feel a bit queasy again, she stopped at the grocery store for some soda crackers. Felt a bit more in control as people smiled at her, wished her a good morning. Treated her like she was normal.

After several crackers and a bottle of water, consumed in her car, she took one last pass by the house. Couldn't tell if Winston was still there or not as the garage was closed. She didn't see movement or lights on, but with the July sun's bright glare on the windows, there could have been either.

First of July. Eight months and twelve days until a new life would enter their world. Eight months and twelve days to figure out what world she or he would be entering. To create a joyful environment for him or her.

At the moment, eight *years* didn't seem long enough to prepare.

She ended up at the Elliott clinic, asking to see Christine.

Emily trusted her.

In a short, short-sleeved denim dress with white lace at the collar and on the buttons up the front, and white tweed wedges, Christine looked both elegant and relaxed. And yet her expression shifted into concern the second she saw Emily, clearly understanding that something was wrong. Which made Emily glad she hadn't gone straight into work.

Judging by the concern on Christine's face, she was doing worse than she'd thought.

"You… Did you lose the baby?" the woman asked even before the office door closed behind them.

"No!" Emily had worn the tight black pin-striped skirt because Winston had liked the amount of leg it showed, but as she sat on the edge of a chair in front of Christine's desk, she had the bizarre thought that she should have worn something more "mother" like. Though what that would be, she had no idea. Mothers didn't stop being women. Sweat trickled down her back—probably leaving a mark on the tapered white blouse.

Like that mattered.

"Winston's alive," she said. And then, at the manager's wide-eyed, openmouthed look, she hurried on with the basic details, leaving out the part about Winston's inability to have sex with her the night before.

Ending with, "He's clearly not happy about the baby. I feel awful. I'm… I thought I was doing the right thing. What he would've wanted. The Winston I knew…he wanted children as badly as I did. He was an only child and couldn't wait to fill our house with…"

Shaking her head, she stopped. "I have no idea what to do."

After a couple of seconds of silence, Christine, who'd taken the seat next to her, asked, "Are you considering terminating the pregnancy?"

"Absolutely not!" She hadn't even thought about it,

but she felt an instinctive horror at the very suggestion. "God, no!" She'd… The idea of ending the life of a child created between her and Winston…

"I'm a little worried, though," she continued. "I was violently sick this morning, and from what I read, morning sickness shouldn't start for another couple of weeks, at least."

"We can get you in to see Dr. Miller this morning, just to ease your mind," Christine said. "But I'm sure everything is fine. It can start as early as two weeks, and with all the stress and shock you've been under for the past forty-eight hours, it's not at all that surprising. Your body is adjusting to a lot, chemically and emotionally."

She nodded, knowing that what Christine said was reasonable, but also that she still wanted to see the doctor. Just to ease her mind. To know what she could do to ease the effects of her stress on the baby. She told Christine that she'd also be calling the chaplain that morning. Planned to do so on her way into LA.

She didn't really need to be there. Bothering the busy woman.

"I just… Do you think I'm selfish? That I did the wrong thing?"

"I think you made the choice that was right for you with the information you had when you made it."

Which didn't really answer her question. And yet, as Christine's words flowed over her, she realized that she'd received the answer she'd needed. She stood, thinking she would wait out in reception until the doctor could see her.

"So…what are you planning to do?" Christine asked, following her to the door.

"Have the baby!" She thought she'd made the completely clear.

"I mean about Winston."

"I'm going to call the chaplain and take it from there. I'm guessing there's counseling for things like this. It's not like he's the first man to come home from captivity. They'll have things to help us adjust and find our way back to normal lie."

"So you plan to let him stay?" They stood at the closed door.

"*Let* him stay? It's his home as much as it is mine. He belongs there…he's not only my husband, he's my soul mate. The love of my life. We'll get through this."

After a long glance, Christine nodded. Pulled open the door. "You've got a lot on your shoulders all of a sudden," she said. "If you ever need to talk, just to vent, you call me. I'm not a certified counselor, but I'm always available to chat."

The offer was professionally made, and yet, as Emily drove from the clinic to LA later that morning, she felt pretty certain that Christine's offer wasn't one she made lightly.

And with that, Emily felt better.

As soon as his session with the anti-terrorist group was done that morning, Winston stopped by the naval legal assistance office.

He absolutely could not be a father. And he couldn't prevent Emily from being a mother—not that he had any intention or desire to do so. But he had to know his legal rights and obligations.

"According to what you've told me, you signed a contract giving her the right to use your sperm for purposes of artificial insemination," Tom Burnett, the base lawyer he'd sought out, told him.

"To specify that she was the only one who could use it," he confirmed.

"Right, but that still gives her the right to use it."

Not what he wanted to hear. Sitting there, in his khakis, talking to a man in dress whites, was not easing his tension any. He needed to be in charge of something, dammit.

Anything.

"Have you asked her to terminate?"

"Hell no!" He didn't even want that. He just…

"Do you have a divorce attorney yet?"

He'd started this conversation by saying that while he and Emily were still legally bound, the marriage was over.

"No," he said. "She doesn't know yet that that's my plan."

The other man nodded. Watched him. He was getting tired of that. Everyone watching him, as though assessing his ability to run his own life.

He'd stayed alive and healthy in enemy territory, living a lie until he could find his way out, a chance to escape. He'd mentally collated two years' worth of intel that he was in the process of regurgitating, and they doubted his ability to conduct his life?

"I suggest, then, that you talk to her," Burnett said. "Really talk to her. And then get an attorney. You have a lot to consider here and there are different ways you could go…"

There. That. "What are those ways?"

"You could try to argue that since your wife used your sperm when you were presumed dead, that she can't now hold you accountable for child support or other paternal responsibilities. In my opinion, you'd have a good case there."

Okay. Good to know. But… "I'll pay child support. I have no problem with that. But the rest of it… The paternal responsibilities…" He had to find a way out of those—couldn't commit to giving his child something he no longer had to offer.

"You could ask the court, as part of the divorce, for shared parenting, for visitation rights or to have your rights severed. I've never actually heard of a parent going to court to have their own rights severed, but your wife could make the request that your rights be severed. If you agree not to fight it, the court would most likely grant her request."

The man listed other options, most of which Winston threw out. They didn't apply to him and Emily. They weren't enemies. Weren't fighting.

They just had to end things.

"Bottom line, you need to talk to her."

The adviser's words played themselves over in his mind as Winston drove from San Diego back to Marie Cove. He wondered about dinner. Thought about using his new smartphone to call Emily and ask if she had anything in mind, but didn't want to bother her at work.

Didn't really want to talk to her at all, at the moment.

She'd gone and used his sperm and gotten herself pregnant. If he was dead, that would probably be pretty cool. Being alive…he just couldn't accept it. Not any of it.

Not her being pregnant.

Not a child with his DNA being born to the world.

Not the major glitch this put in his plan to set her free and get on with the rest of his life as a naval police officer, serving others, protecting them, not hurting them.

Serving, protecting. That was what he was good at.

He'd get there. It was the plan. He just had to factor in an unforeseen detour.

Emily stopped at the grocery store again on the way home from work. She'd told Steve that Winston was home, and he'd insisted that she leave early. And take the next day off. He was stepping in personally to handle her accounts. She'd texted Winston to let him know when she'd be at the house.

Maybe he'd be there. Maybe her warning would give him a chance to vacate. Either way, they'd get through it.

She'd told others at work about his return and every single one of them had been overjoyed for her. They'd shown concern, of course, for Winston, seeming to know that they had some tough times in the immediate future. But all in all, it was a joyous day. A couple of her coworkers had hugged her. Matilda, her account assistant, had cried.

She'd cried, too. A couple of times. And then she got to work. Winston and the baby needed her to be strong.

And life was a gift. Winston had some issues, they had some struggles ahead of them, but he was alive and he was home! Every life had struggles.

Not many had a life come back from the grave!

And with the baby already on the way, she was blessed beyond her wildest imaginings.

With a pound of their favorite broccoli salad from the deli, she pulled into the garage, figuring she'd broil some chicken for dinner. She smelled something wonderful when she walked in the door.

"You're grilling!" she said, setting her bag, along with the grocery sack, on the counter to take a peek out the sliding glass door that led from the dining room to their backyard.

She hadn't been in their paved grilling gazebo other than to clean it since he left.

"I had to change out the propane tank, but everything else was fine."

Had he almost just smiled at her?

He was still in his uniform khakis. Must have just gotten home a little bit before her. And he was making dinner! She loved his chicken. Her mouth was already watering.

"I brought broccoli salad," she told him, pulling out the container. And then opened the refrigerator door to see that he'd done the same. It was as though they'd been of the same mind. Others might see something spectacular, weird or otherworldly about that.

Emily smiled.

To her, it just said that Winston was home.

Ten minutes after she got there, Emily was sitting down to dinner with her husband. She'd set the table while he brought the chicken and potatoes in from the grill. She got drinks. He put the broccoli salad out. They didn't touch. Didn't talk much.

And she felt so happy, so excited, that she could barely contain herself.

Over dinner she told him about her day, starting with the new account she'd signed. She asked him how his meeting had gone. His one-word response, "fine," didn't deflate her good mood.

Things weren't going to just suddenly be normal overnight. His suffering and the repercussions from it were real. But she could still find joy in small steps along the way.

"You're eating well," he said, while she gave herself the pep talk. And she was excited all over again. He was paying attention. Seemed to care.

So Winston.

"I feel fine," she told him.

He nodded. Gave her a long look, and she held her breath, thinking he'd mention the baby. When he didn't, she went back to eating.

He knew about the baby; that was the important thing. And he was there.

The rest would come.

Taking her cue from his personal comment, she told him that she'd let everyone at work know that he was back. She relayed their reactions and the personal good wishes to him that had been offered as well.

He forked the last bite of food on his plate. Chewed it. Swallowed.

And said, "I've been advised to tell you that I need a divorce."

Chapter Ten

There was just no easy way to present it. He'd worked on it all afternoon and determined that the kindest thing was the old "ripping off the bandage" strategy. Do it quickly and get it over with. It seemed to hurt less that way.

At least the pain was swifter. So, presumably, one could get past it quicker.

Emily's fork clattered against her plate, off the edge of the table, onto the floor. The hand that had been holding it was shaking. Pushing aside an urge to hold that hand, knowing that it was just programmed reaction left over from his years with her, he picked up her fork. Set it on the table.

His movement seemed to spur her into action. Jumping up, fork in hand, she went to the sink. Rinsed the fork. Pulled a paper towel off the roll. Dried the fork. Threw the paper towel away, carried the fork back to the table.

Put it on her plate. Those long legs, in that skirt… In a former day he'd have pulled her onto his lap.

Emily picked up her plate and carried it to the sink. She'd changed her mind about using the fork she'd cleaned? Needed her plate cleaned, too? She'd eaten all of the broccoli salad and most of her chicken. More than half of the potatoes.

Leaving her plate at the sink, she came back to the table. He expected her to take his plate next. Cleaning the kitchen hardly seemed urgent at the moment, but if that was what she wanted to do, he wouldn't stop her. Had to give her whatever time and space she needed.

He wasn't going to push her. He had six months. And they had a lot to get through.

He wouldn't push, anyway. She was pregnant, for God's sake.

When his memory provided a sudden flash of his early-morning minutes with Emily in the spare bathroom, he swore silently. He'd just given her stress right after she'd eaten. Bad timing, that.

Leaving his empty plate in front of him, Emily sat back down. Folded her hands on the table in front of her. She'd curled her hair that morning, and the long blond strands touched the tops of her wrists, even with her sitting up straight.

Those ends would be silky soft. A whisper on skin.

"Who advised you?"

Not the conversation he'd expected.

He'd told her he'd answer any question honestly.

"A legal advocate."

"When?"

"Today."

"You sought legal advice today?"

"Yes."

"So…you already have an attorney?"

"No." But perhaps he should have acquired one before having this discussion. He only now saw how it would have strengthened his position to have done so.

She was frowning. "I'm confused," she said. "Why would a legal advocate advise you to get a divorce? You've been home less than two days. I called Chaplain Blaine today. She said that we can't know anything just yet, in terms of what our future will look like. She said right now the only thing we can give ourselves is time. And counseling, too, of course."

Expecting patience to settle over him—an emotion he knew and trusted—Winston was surprised by the instant flood of exactly the opposite coursing through him. He was antsy.

Emily was going to be hurt worse the longer this continued. What right did anyone have to hurt this beautiful, giving woman any more than was necessary?

What right did he have to come barreling in without sensitivity enough to give her time to accept the inevitable?

"She's right, of course," he said, as patience finally settled over him.

Emily's frown grew. "I don't get it…why would a legal adviser tell you you need a divorce?" And with a shake of her head, added, "Why did you even seek out his advice?"

It was all one and the same, wasn't it? He was obligated to give her the most honest answer. Thinking back over his day, he had to admit… "He didn't tell me I needed a divorce," he said slowly, remembering the man's exact words. "He said I needed to talk to you. Really talk."

Face clearing, Emily sat back. "Okay, so talk."

He pushed his plate aside, leaned forward, his arms on the table now. Would have liked to loosen his collar, his tie. But knew that when everything was spinning out of control, whatever protocol he could hold on to kept him sane.

He didn't know for sure how much she knew. How much they'd told her. But suddenly saw how important it was that she hear it from him.

She'd see the change in him, given the time they'd both now been advised to take, but she might see it sooner if she knew how it had come about. Why.

She had a right to know.

Someday, that child would need to know.

"We were ambushed by a small community of militants not far from where we'd set up camp." He didn't have to give minute details. The bodies falling. All guys he knew. Every single one of them. The blood spurts.

Closing his eyes, he shut out the picture. This was an exercise he had down pat. A challenge he'd met and conquered.

"There were seven of us left, including my sergeant."

"Sergeant Dane Somersby?"

Taken aback, he stared at her. "Yes, how did you know?"

"He sent me a letter, after you'd been declared… dead…" Her voice caught and she stopped. But didn't take her gaze from his. She looked him right in the eye. That's how they'd been since the first day they'd met. A lifetime ago.

Hard to believe he'd ever been fourteen.

"He said you saved his life…"

So she did know. At least some of it.

"Did he tell you how?"

She shook her head, her gaze almost pleading. She needed this.

Something he could actually give her.

"I turned traitor."

Pulling back, she blinked. Frowned. Shook her head. "No way." Then shook her head more fiercely. "I will never believe that, Winston. Come up with whatever stories you must, but don't insult me with lies."

He almost smiled. Could feel a small appreciative hint of humor inside him. That quickly faded away. "Dust in the Wind."

The old song from his father's day had become a mantra, living over there in the Afghan desert.

"For all intents and purposes, I became a traitor," he modified his words. "The way we were ambushed…it seemed probable that someone on their side had infiltrated us somehow. We were sitting ducks. So I went AWOL. Left without anyone knowing, without orders. We had no idea where or how they were getting our intel, so I couldn't afford to tell anyone."

"If there was a traitor of the US side, he'd have shared your plan with the enemy, and the men who were honorable, would never have allowed you to go."

Right. He'd forgotten how often she'd been traveling along his same thought process. The memory didn't bring comfort. Just made it all harder.

And more necessary to get the job done.

"I hid out in the desert for a day, and then, with my uniform shirt on a stick, went walking into their little village. I'd seen a group of kids playing and stayed close to them, figuring that they wouldn't shoot and risk hitting one of them. In their own perspective they're a lot like us. Loyal. Protective of their own."

But he was getting off course.

"Long story short, I gave them enough information to convince them that I wanted to be one of them. And then gave them enough false information to allow my comrades time to get out. I knew a group of friendlies were close, I just had to provide distraction so they could get to my guys. After my goal was met. All I had to do was wait for a chance to escape. And in the meantime, I figured that I'd spend my days gathering intel, in the event I actually made it out. And every other day, it seemed, I was given another challenge. Something else I had to do to show my loyalty. That first day, I had to kill a soldier, one from the US side, and bring him to them."

That had been a choice where he'd crossed another line. Turning over one his comrades.

The look of horror on her face came and went quickly. Its existence at all was confirmation of what he knew. There were just some things a man did from which he couldn't come back.

The fact that he even could...

"Winston." Her hand touched his arm. Softly. She left it there, her fingers slowly moving against his skin.

"I, uh, before I'd entered their camp...after I went AWOL... I knew where one of our men had been stationed and slaughtered. I found him. Put on his bloody uniform, dressed him in mine. Just that easily, I became Private First Class Danny Garrison. The kid...he'd been born to an older couple who doted on him. Who'd been so afraid for him to deploy. And yet he'd been the most willing, most dedicated of all of us. I admired the hell out of him. Of all the deaths that had happened that week, his…"

No. He stopped talking.

She only needed the facts. No sense making things messier than they had to be. Clouding things prolonged the inevitable. He knew this. Had survived by it.

"I knew I was walking into eventual death." He looked her right in the eye when he admitted the god-awful truth. He'd been willing to leave her, to do something that his job hadn't even required him to do.

That had been a choice that changed everything.

"And knew that when it was all over, the man who'd walked into that enemy village would likely be hailed as a hero. I wanted that for Danny's parents. So I moved his body away from his designated post to a place I'd more likely have been, having gone AWOL. He was pretty mutilated. Cause of death was clear. It was unlikely an autopsy would be done."

"That makes no sense, Winston. Recovered military bodies are sent to Dover, identified by fingerprints and dental records."

Of course she'd know that. He had, too.

"When you're over there…" He shook his head. Trying to make someone a hero by giving him credit for something that you were ashamed of having done?

No, wait. He wasn't at all ashamed of what he'd done. He'd saved lives of men he knew. And now, with the far-reaching effects of what he'd learned, who knew how many more would be saved?

He'd done the right thing.

Just not something the Winston Hannigan who'd left California, who'd been married to Emily Hannigan, would have done.

Danny hadn't had a wife or kids. The choice would have made his parents proud.

"His face was... There wouldn't have been enough for dental records," he said. "But you're right, if I died, as expected, the US military likely would have been able to identify me."

The navy—and the special ground force operators—thought he'd made a smart choice, posing as an already-dead soldier. To protect his own future. The enemy combatants with whom he'd lived had likely never heard of Petty Officer First Class Winston Hannigan.

And by using Danny that way...

Maybe he'd hope to ensure, as best as he could, that his uniform would be found, that Emily would be notified right away, to save her the angst of not knowing...

As though a light had been shut off, Winston went to a dark place inside. A place he'd discovered within himself during his time in that desert. He spent a lot of time there. It was quiet. Peaceful.

Thoughts came more clearly. He'd detoured off point. He went back.

"When I was ordered, as a sign of sovereignty, to deliver up a body, it was as though what I'd done with Danny had been preordained. I went to the body I'd left sitting up against a tree, in my own uniform. He'd been dead less than twenty-four hours. From a distance, I shot it without hesitation. Multiple times. With a couple of my new 'brothers' looking on. Then I walked alone up to that pile of mutilated flesh on the ground, lifted it up against me, carried it all the way back to the village and gave it to them."

He'd delivered up Danny's body, preventing the young

man's parents from ever having his body back. From having a proper burial.

But not before he'd ripped off the top left of the shirt Danny had been wearing, leaving his own identifiers for anyone to find in what was the site of an obvious massacre.

He'd done it all. One thought leading to the next.

"If you'd been killed in the village, I was told that chances were the insurgents would have sent your uniform, or some kind of identifier, as a taunt, but they'd have destroyed the body," Emily said.

Which would have made Danny the hero.

They may or may not have sent the uniform. If he'd been killed in that village, chances were his body—and uniform—would have ended up in a burn pit. There were a lot of ifs. Some more sound than others. Just like his thinking that day in the desert, when he'd known he'd never see Emily again.

And maybe changing identities with Danny hadn't been his best thinking.

The fact that, even so, Emily had followed the train of thought bothered him.

But this—him being here with her—wasn't about him.

"Killing" Danny, handing over his body, hadn't been the only life-altering thing they'd required of him. It was enough, though, to show Emily that some changes were irrevocable—the price one paid for the choices one made.

No need to tell her more—to hurt her in a way that would change her forever, too. As long as the goal was met—as long as she was free to move on to a happy life—his job would be done.

When he realized that her hand was still on his arm, because she squeezed it, he moved. Sat back.

"It's just going to take time, Winston," she said softly. "The longer you're here, living your normal life…the sting will become more manageable. And you'll start to see things from a different perspective."

What the hell? She was a counselor now? Or parroting what she'd heard from whoever all she'd called that day? A bout of frustration spewed before he could stop it.

"Why does everyone seem to think I don't know my own mind?"

"I can't speak for everyone else. I just know you. The way you reacted over there, it's what I would expect from you, Win. You were in an untenable situation. With people dying around you. You'd had a few weeks' training in ground combat…"

He wanted none of it.

"Can you just do one thing for me?" she asked.

"What?" He didn't know if he hoped he could or couldn't at that point.

"Can you just give this all some time? Wait on the whole lawyer conversation. We don't even need to talk about the baby. Just give us some time."

What choice did he have? He needed her happy.

And everyone was telling him the same thing. Take some time. Give it time. No one seemed to get that he'd just given it two excruciatingly long years. He needed to live his life. And to make that happen, bottom line—he had to follow orders.

"How much time?"

Her shrug, the expression on her face…he recognized it. She was laying her heart open to him, not laying down the law.

"I'm guessing you'll know," she said now. "Or I will."

The plan would work better with a set period. A date.

But he didn't want to put it out further than she'd need. She was the one who had to figure out that they weren't going to work. He was already there.

"Fine," he said. Mentally giving her three months, tops. Until they at least revisited the conversation. He needed time on the other end to get a lawyer and get divorced before his six-month leave was up.

Chapter Eleven

I've been advised to tell you I need a divorce. Emily closed her eyes, then opened them again, focusing on the computer in front of her, willing herself to block Winston's words from her brain. She'd been told to take a few days off, but that didn't mean she couldn't work from home. Concentrating on campaign strategies, convincing news and television sources that her clients' information was of interest to them, working out print advertising deals that were the most financially beneficial, gave her mind something productive to focus on. Well…mostly productive. Coming up with ways to reach consumers in a world overloaded with media and fake news. With one of her current products, she'd been in meetings with retailers to convince them to at least give a chance to her new and inventive way to make in-store advertising more effective.

Winston had gone out to the garage after their dinner conversation. She'd heard him at his workbench. Opening drawers. Reacquainting himself with his tools? Or cataloging their value for a fair split of marital property?

No. She couldn't afford to get maudlin. The week before she'd been a widow. Today she was a wife. Bleak could turn into miraculous in an instant.

Winston needed time. She couldn't take anything he said right then as absolute gospel. It wouldn't be fair to him to do so.

And their baby… If she'd known he was alive, there was no way she'd have had herself inseminated. He was struggling enough, working through two years of his life lived in a way he never would have chosen without being forced, trying to find himself in the life he'd left behind. Adding a baby into that…

No matter how wonderful that news…even in a normal, blessed life, there were moments of doubt. And some anxiety over the irrevocable changes that were coming.

Not only would he be responsible for himself, but she'd landed the responsibilities of fatherhood on his shoulders.

And yet…she was pregnant! And Winston was home! For a woman who'd been bereft and completely alone just weeks before, the universe had clearly gifted her.

So, what was it worth to her? Was she going to buckle at the first sign of challenge? The first obstacle?

Hell no, she was not. She was going to be a dedicated partner to her husband who was struggling. And a good parent to the baby growing inside her. She was going to be the woman in this family. Loving them. Holding them all together.

Including herself.

She'd heard the door into the kitchen open and close.

Winston had stopped by the entry to the office. If he'd asked, there was no way she could have told him what she was staring at on her screen.

"You can come in," she said. "I've kept your computer updated."

"I don't want to bother your work."

"You used to be at your desk a lot when I was in here working and it never bothered me. That hasn't changed." How did she know that until they'd tried?

She slowed herself down. Giving him platitudes, or throwing out anything that could be construed as barbs, whether they'd been meant that way or not, was not the way to help her marriage.

"At least, I can't imagine it would," she clarified. "Truthfully, it would probably help. I spent a lot of hours sitting here unable to focus because of the emptiness over there." She nodded toward his desk.

When he still hesitated, she knew not to push. Instead, she x-ed out of her work network. "I'm done for the night anyway," she said as he remained in the doorway.

Something on his mind?

Why else would he still be standing there?

Preparing herself not to take whatever he said personally, to remember he was in a transition frame of mind, she remembered something.

"I didn't tell you, I'm off work for the next couple of days. Boss's orders." She'd meant to tell him at dinner. Got sidetracked by the divorce advice. That had turned out not to be that at all, she reminded herself. The advice had been to talk to her.

He'd taken that to the extreme.

Standing there in his khakis, top button still fastened, hands in his pockets, he looked…so damned good to her.

Exactly as he'd looked so many times in the past, stopping by the door on his way into work on the days she'd been working from home. If he weighed less, had scars… anything…maybe it would be easier to remember that he wasn't whole. Yet.

Not that she wished in any way, for any second, that he'd been physically harmed. She was grateful as all hell that he'd devised a plan that had actually allowed him to save the rest of the troops in his unit and keep his own body intact.

Unchanged.

Except…the episode in bed last night came back to her. Winston's sexual…inability. She'd lain awake, fighting tears, completely shocked, the night before. Until she'd thought of how it must be affecting him, instead of her. For some reason an old episode of *Friends* came to her… A character who'd been highly sexed had been unable to get it up for his soon-to-be-wife. He'd been hugely out of whack, fearing there was something grossly wrong with him. There hadn't been. He'd been as randy as ever soon after.

The show was a farce—and maybe the episode popping into her brain a sign that she'd spent too much time streaming old sitcoms over the past two years—but the effect on a man of being unable to perform…that was very real.

She hadn't mentioned the episode to Chaplain Blaine. But figured that it would be dealt with in counseling at some point, if necessary.

Wanting to ask him about going to someone together, she took a look at his nondescript expression, the hands in his pockets, and figured another time would be better.

Time. It was all about time. And timing.

Like the fact that she'd been inseminated seemingly at the same time that Winston was crawling his way out of the desert.

There were no mistakes.

And him standing there...when bedtime loomed...

The man was hot. He'd tripped her trigger from the moment she'd had a trigger to trip. But...

"I'd like to ask one thing of you, if I may."

He cocked his head, watching her. She took that as his agreement to consider her request.

"Sex is completely your call. When, or if, it happens between us again is totally up to you." His jutted chin could have been him biting his tongue, so to speak. Or acknowledging appreciation. She'd figure out how to read this new Winston, she just needed a little time.

Time again. At least they had it now. A month ago...

"But I'd like to request that we at least sleep in the same room. In the same bed, unless there's some reason you need to sleep on the floor. Or...something."

She'd heard of that. Being a military wife brought exposure to some horror stories.

"I don't think..."

"Please, Winston." She cut him off. "We've said we're going to give this time. But if you're going to act as though we're already apart, then you aren't really giving us any time at all. You're just humoring 'us.' In which case, you might as well just pack up and leave."

Oh God. She wanted the words back. Instantly.

If he walked out on her... Just... Shit.

She'd said she wouldn't push, and now she just had. But as she waited for his response, she had to admit to herself that she stood by what she said. If he wasn't open to possibility, him being there was a farce. Didn't mean he couldn't come back, when he'd had time to get himself together, but it meant there was no point in him being there then.

"I'll sleep in the bed." As he issued the statement he turned and headed down the hall to their room. He didn't say "our room." Or "our bed." She caught the gentle distinction in his word choice. Knew him well enough to know that he'd chosen it deliberately. He'd definitely changed some. But deep down, Winston was there. She was seeing signs of him even now.

Recognizing things. Like she'd just known about his choice of words being deliberate. But she caught a significance he might not have. If he was really and truly already out the door, he'd have said, "your room." Or "your bed."

With a grin on her face, she went in behind him to get ready for bed. Hopefully he'd have the TV on. Give them a chance to lie there and unwind without the need for interaction.

If he didn't, she wouldn't push again.

But it would be a damned long night.

She was going to bed wide-awake.

He'd forgotten just how sharp Emily was. Not that he'd thought her slow, at all. He knew she was intelligent. But he'd forgotten about her acute ability to hear what wasn't being said.

That was a major fail on his part. The kind of mistake that could blow an entire plan. Make the difference between failure and success.

Over the next few days he coexisted with her, leaving for the base first thing in the morning and returning in time to help with dinner in the evening. He had no real need to be at the base that long. When someone wanted to interview him, he could be busy for an hour or two. Otherwise he worked out. Watched training videos and actual exercises. He went to the library and read everything there was to know about naval police life.

In the evenings, after dinner, he did more of the same. Researched. Read.

Started to get a little bored. And then his mind, craving stimulation, began to segue into useless questions.

Emily's perfume, for instance. What made it so noticeable? And why hadn't it been as obvious in the past? He knew it was the same stuff she'd always worn because he'd actually checked it out in the bathroom one morning after his shower.

He googled olfactory glands one night. Didn't find anything of pertinent use.

Searched morning sickness, too, although as far as he knew, Emily hadn't been sick other than that one time. What he read told him too much and nothing at all. Some women got it. Some didn't. Some had it violently, some mildly. Sometimes, it came within the first two weeks. More generally it happened around the sixth week. Some had it throughout the pregnancy. A lot didn't.

He paid a bit more attention when he read that some women actually had to be hospitalized because of it if they weren't able to keep enough down to get proper nutrition. If she started to puke again, and it became clear that him being there was causing the stress that made it happen, he'd insist on staying elsewhere. Even if that delayed the culmination of his plan.

The last thing he wanted was her in the hospital. She needed to be healthy and strong or she wasn't going to be happy.

On Friday of that first week back in Marie Cove, he came home to find Emily in the kitchen, stirring a big pan of kielbasa, green beans and potatoes—one of his favorites—and talking on the phone. She got off almost as soon as he came in.

"'Bye, Mom, love you!"

Shock hit him flat in the face. Which sent a spiral of panic through him that he quickly obliterated with conscious reminders that he had nothing to fear except being afraid. He'd proven he could trust himself to handle anything else.

"How was your day?" Emily's question, aimed at him, though she hadn't turned around, helped put his world right—bringing him fully out of the places down deep that could kill a guy if he couldn't get out.

Of course she'd be talking to her mother. He should have asked about the woman. And his own parents... He'd put off telling them he'd been found, but his superiors had made it clear that they'd only hold off on official announcements to secondary family for a short period.

The short period was probably up. The fact that he hadn't given much thought to either his parents or Emily's mom and brother bothered him. A lot.

He cared about them all. Took for granted that they'd be there when he was ready. But why hadn't he asked about them? Or needed to know what had transpired in their lives over the past couple of years?

"I was told my folks are still in Florida," he said to Emily's back. The pot didn't need to be stirred continuously. An occasional swipe over the couple of hours the stew would cook was enough. And yet she hadn't turned around.

"They are." In another one of her short-skirted suits—

navy this time—and those three-inch heels that had always drawn his attention straight to her calves—she'd obviously started dinner as soon as she'd come in from work.

"And doing well, I presume? Since you haven't said otherwise?"

"I haven't spoken to them since a week after you were declared officially dead," she told him. "But they were doing fine then. Your dad's golfing five days a week in a men's league. And your mom's involved with a women's political group. Doing some rallies, making signs. Having a lot of lunches with the girls."

They were coping, he translated. A new weight settled on him. Not so much a need as an awareness. He should call them.

Should want to see them.

He didn't, really.

Which kind of bothered him. But not as much as it should have. When parts of you were dead to self, when you knew that duty was stronger than so-called love or the pull of family ties, you were free of some of the confines that emotions put on you.

He should put a call to them on the schedule, though.

"And your Mom?"

"Still in San Diego with Michael. Jamie's six now and Dylan is seven. They're getting involved in school activities and keeping her busy."

Michael. The brother-in-law who had once been like a brother to him. Again...that shock shot through him that he'd given so little thought to them all. It just didn't seem right.

His in-laws lived about forty-five minutes south from the base where he spent his time, in a suburb, not really

San Diego proper, but still…they were a lot closer than Florida and…

"Does she know I'm back?"

"Of course not. I told you I wouldn't tell anyone, other than the people at work, until you were ready. You know that once we do there'll be a deluge of activity."

"Not if we tell them we need some time. They'll respect that."

Something he should have seen before. Tended to. The sudden consciousness confused him.

Shrugging it off, Winston figured he'd had enough on his plate the past week, what with having to move back in with Emily and finding out that she was pregnant. He could be forgiven for a lapse or two.

"We should call them all," he said now. And then had another thought. "Do they know about the baby yet?"

When Emily turned, he was struck by the look in her eyes as her gaze met his. The depth there…

He could almost sense it calling to him, saying something…but whatever it was, he couldn't quite hear. And knew better than to try. Getting caught up in the fantasy would only bring unmeasurable pain. For both of them.

"I haven't told anyone about the baby except you," she said, leaning back against the counter. "I want to wait until the first trimester passes safely."

She wanted to know she wasn't going to miscarry. Because while he was sitting around looking up olfactory glands, she'd been worrying about the baby she carried. Caring deeply about it.

He was pretty sure that made him a schmuck. Something he'd already figured out about himself.

"So…you want to call them separately or together? To tell them I'm alive, I mean."

Tears sprang to her eyes. She reached for his hand. "Together, of course."

He saw the mistake too late, giving her that choice. Leading her to believe that there was a possibility of "together" for them.

It was a mistake he couldn't make again.

Chapter Twelve

Funny how when time stood still, it still flew by. Days that were mostly the same passed, one after another, broken up by cacophony on the weekends as her family and Winston's parents descended upon them. Emily'd known his assertion that they'd give them time was ludicrous. Had figured he'd known it, too. And yet he'd seemed completely shocked when, after their initial phone calls, there were a flurry of texts and more calls—including video calls—as arrangements were made for everyone to visit Marie Cove.

With her mom and brother and the kids it was both easier and harder, because they could just drive up and be there. And they had, the Saturday morning after their Friday night calls. They'd had an hour's notice, during which Winston had gone into their room dressed in his khakis and come out wearing a pair of blue shorts and an off-white button-down shirt. It was the first time she'd seen him in anything but pajama bottoms or his uniform since he'd walked back into her world. She'd had to excuse herself to the bathroom to wipe away tears and calm her pounding heart.

They'd met her brother's car out in the driveway, standing there together, though not touching. It had both filled her heart and broken it, as they all had the reunion she'd often imagined for Winston's return. He'd played his part in front the family. Giving her long looks, referring to her often, staying close to her.

And then they'd be gone and so would he—the part of him that was her loving husband, happy to be back in the home he'd "built" with her. In his stead would be the calm, unemotional though overall kind version of Winston she was coming to know.

The following weekend his parents had been there. They'd tried to insist on coming immediately, the previous Friday when they'd received the call, but they'd been better about listening to Winston's request for time. They'd given him the week.

And so it went, one week following another. During the week they'd work, him in San Diego, her in LA, unless either of them had a work-from-home day, which they'd coordinate to make certain that they weren't both there at the same time. On the weekends, either his parents flew in, or her mother, at least, drove up, and then they'd go to the beach, eat out, do a little trail walking— or even just stream movies. Winston had missed two years' worth of TV and movies, and her mother made it her mission to see that he got caught up on anything anyone might be talking about so he didn't feel lost. And she'd also insisted on cooking him every meal she'd ever made for him that he'd said he liked.

As much as Emily normally craved her independence, she was hugely grateful to have her mother around.

The warm family weekends fortified her for the rest of the week, when Winston largely withdrew into himself again.

She'd mentioned counseling several times. Had had phone sessions with a woman referred to her by Chaplain Blaine. Each time she'd suggested they go together, he let her know that his own sessions were enough for him.

And she'd gone to the clinic to see Christine. Just to chat. And had had her first scheduled visit with Dr. Miller, who would be delivering her baby. So far, so good. After that first bout of morning sickness, there'd been nothing more than a few queasy moments taken care of by the soda crackers she kept in her bag. And Dr. Miller said everything looked great.

The nursery was currently nonexistent. Their guests stayed in the spare bedroom that she'd been about to turn into the baby's haven. And since none of them knew about the baby yet…

Sometimes, on her drives to and from work, when she wasn't rethinking every nuance of every moment spent with Winston, looking for signs of change, trying to understand and find patience, she played around with baby names. But she always came up empty. Maybe once she knew if it was a boy or a girl.

Maybe when Winston was in a place to have the discussion with her. This was his baby, too—their baby. She didn't want to choose a name alone.

Her stomach hadn't changed in appearance at all that she could see. Standing in her bathroom one Thursday

night the second week of August, studying her nearly
naked form in bikini briefs before pulling on her nightgown, she was hard-pressed to believe she really was
pregnant.

Life had become one incredibly long surreal day that
just kept repeating itself.

"Is something wrong?"

Jumping so rapidly she hit her wrist on the granite
countertop, Emily turned and stared at Winston.

"I didn't hear you come in," she told him, noting his
frown. They had a routine. She got into bed, and a few
minutes later he came in. They either had the TV on or
not. He'd turn his back and they'd go to sleep. Never
touching under the covers. Ever. At all.

She'd broken the routine with the extra time she'd
taken to stand there and look at herself.

He glanced at her wrist. "Is it okay?"

Flipping her hand back and forth, she showed him the
wrist still worked. And then grabbed her nightgown. Pulling it over breasts that ached for his touch.

He'd looked at them—her breasts. When he'd first
come in. She'd seen the surreptitious glance. Warmth
was flooding her lower parts. Even now, after all of these
weeks of stoicism. The fact both pleased and bothered
her.

Because nothing was just one way or the other these
days.

Nothing made sense.

And nothing was clear.

Emily standing nearly naked in the bathroom, looking
at herself. For the next couple of days Winston couldn't

get that moment to leave him alone. He'd send it off and it came back. Again and again.

Her mom was in town, which made things easier for him. She didn't see him as well as his own folks did. Didn't look as hard, he figured. Mostly, he just had to act around her as he'd acted before Afghanistan and she was happy.

Keeping Emily's mom happy was important to the plan.

Not that he'd been "acting" in the past. He'd been sincerely living what he'd believed to be true. But propriety had meant he couldn't act on all his impulses and emotions back then. He couldn't say whatever thoughts might occur to him—not when anyone else had been around. Or grab her up and kiss her. Haul her off to bed. Or out on an adventure. No, when others were around, he'd always had to filter. Figured most couples did.

Being removed was a way of life now. Real life. He just had to touch Emily when others were there, because they'd find it odd if he didn't, which would create complications neither of them wanted or needed. Touching in front of others couldn't lead to anything more as others were right there. So there was no threat to the plan in doing so.

But her staring at herself as she had…there was a threat there. He just couldn't find it. What had been wrong? Had she been to the doctor? Heard some bad news?

Dear God, had she lost the baby? And not told him? Wouldn't he notice something like that? She'd be in the hospital, right? Or lying in bed at home?

There'd been a girl in their high school who'd been said to have had a baby at home and come to school that same day. She hadn't even told anyone she was pregnant.

She'd been a big girl, but Winston had never quite believed the rumor. Emily had. Still...

They didn't ever mention Emily's child. At all. But he figured she was taking care of herself. And it. The child. Doing whatever she needed to be doing at that stage. Seeing the doctor. Eating what she'd been told to eat, not that he'd noticed any real change in her diet, other than the coffee.

He hadn't seen her taking vitamins, either, though he remembered his sister-in-law, her brother's ex-wife, complaining about the horse pills she had to get down every day. She'd complained about stretch marks, too. So maybe that was it? Emily had been checking for marks?

On Sunday after Emily's mom left and before dinner, when Emily was doing a load of laundry, he quickly searched online for information about miscarriages. And found, as before, it could go any number of ways. A woman could have a miscarriage, not tell anyone and go on with her day. Almost like a monthly cycle, apparently, as early on as Emily was.

Or she could be hospitalized with hemorrhaging.

And there were many many scenarios in between.

How in the hell did one do this? Have a baby with any kind of strategy? The parameters were so broad there was no way to prepare for all eventualities.

He was still in a flux over the whole thing when he crawled into bed, as far from her as he could get, later that night. The television was on. Streaming an old sitcom rerun. He tried to focus only on it. To relax his muscles, one section of the body at a time, as he'd trained himself to do. To allow sleep to take him long enough to rejuvenate his assets.

He couldn't do that until her breathing settled. It was

wrong for him to go to sleep if she was bothered enough to stay awake. He was there to help her get through this, to find the new reality, and then be able to find her happiness. One thing was certain for Winston: he didn't sleep on the job.

"Is everything okay? Physically?" His voice reverberated with the force of a gunshot to him, breaking the silence as it did. Talking in bed wasn't part of their current procedure.

There'd been something displeased about the way she'd been looking at her belly—not that he saw anything distressing there. A little bit of shape, firm, gorgeous as it had always been.

"Physically?" She turned her head to look at him, her long blond hair a halo around her pillow, framing her face with the TV casting light and dark shadows over her. He couldn't make out the blue of her eyes, but recognized the way they'd just softened.

Off course. Off course. Off course.

"With the...child you're carrying," he quickly veered back. Finding the whole situation too damned awkward. What did he call it? Pregnancy seemed too...personal... though he couldn't say why. And baby... Yeah, everything about that gave him the cold sweats. Add the "our" to it that he feared she was doing in her own mind, and he would be out of bed and on his way to San Diego on foot in his pajamas.

She blinked but didn't turn away. "Yes," she said, a little smile forming on her lips. "It's great, actually. Dr. Miller says that so far, we're perfect." She met his gaze... that look back again, only different, too. Something new—even for the old "them." "Our first ultrasound is in a couple of weeks. If the baby's presenting right, we'll know if we're having a boy or a girl. You're welcome to come along if you'd like." She named the date and time. A Wednesday, more than a week away.

He thought about it. Because a soldier needed all bases covered, a leader needed to gather as many firsthand facts as possible, and a protector had to understand the risks.

Then he pictured himself standing in a small examination room with Emily lying on the table.

"Technology has improved so much," she said softly. "You can really make things out a lot more clearly now than you used to be able to do."

As in, a small arm, or leg, as opposed to a blob on a screen?

He turned over, giving her his back.

"Winston? I'd like you to come."

Oh God. What was a man supposed to do when being decent just didn't seem to be working?

"I'll see what I can do," he told her. Honesty was all he had.

And he honestly couldn't envision a time when he'd be standing in that room, with Emily on the table, looking at that screen. There was absolutely no contingency for such an action.

In spite of the meeting he had at the base the next morning—discussing intel, giving his opinion as to possible reaction against potential strategies, just based on what he'd seen and heard—he lay awake a long time, pondering action items. Seeking internal approval or rejection. He'd mentally given their current situation three months and had no way of knowing if they would be enough.

Emily was changing…he could see it in little ways. The calm that sometimes replaced her usual positive outlook. Fewer tears. The way she gave him room when he passed her, making sure they didn't touch.

The way she never looked at him when others were around and they did touch.

Her ability to fall into a completely platonic routine with him.

She was getting it. He was sure of it.

Until she'd looked at him in bed that night. Was she just camouflaging for his sake? Exhibiting more of that unending patience she'd always had? Hiding her inexhaustible hope on his behalf?

Time was doing one helluva lousy job taking care of things.

Eventually, with the television still droning softly in the distance, he fell asleep. But awoke again, instantly awake, some time later. Because of the TV? He reached for the remote on the headboard. Clicked off the TV before his eyes were fully open, and froze. The movement, he now realized had awoken him, was a problem. A big problem.

He was in bed with Emily. And hard as a rock.

He'd been dreaming. Rubbing whipped cream on Emily's belly so that it didn't get stretch marks. Or something.

So far, he'd mastered mind-over-body with precision, preventing himself from reacting sexually when he was close to her. The ease with which he'd completed the task had actually been a blessing.

And now his mind was turning traitor on him?

That was a complication he did not need.

Chapter Thirteen

It was the little things. Her mother had always told her, pay attention to the little things and usually the bigger ones would fall into place.

She was trying. God, she was trying.

She'd spend the rest of her life with the current version of Winston, if that was all that was left of the man she loved, but it was taking its toll.

Not nearly the toll he'd paid, though, losing two years of his life in the Afghan desert. Still, as almost another week passed and the ultrasound loomed only five days away, she drove home Friday knowing that something had to give—at least a little. Either her hope or his reticence. They were facing the first weekend home alone since his return. And they hadn't even discussed what those two days might look like.

Would he be going to the base? Doing whatever he

did there, besides working out? And it wasn't like he'd even told her he was doing that. She'd seen him carry his gym bag into the house and throw the clothes in the washer. His uniforms, he took to the cleaners. The rest of his clothes she'd washed with hers just as she always had.

She was trying so hard not to push him, but dang, nothing seemed to be changing. They were living in a stagnant unrealistic world that wasn't going to be a healthy environment in which to bring a baby.

If only she'd waited a couple of weeks to have herself inseminated. While in the beginning, she'd thought the timing to be the universe taking care of them, she was edging more toward darker thoughts these days—finding the timing almost cruel.

For everyone.

Winston's car was already in the garage when she pulled in, ready for, if not a showdown, at least some kind of meaningful conversation.

And at the very least, to find out once and for all if her baby's father would be accompanying her to the ultrasound five days hence.

Letting herself into the kitchen with a strong reminder to herself not to push, but to maybe gently lead a little, she was surprised by the stillness. No dinner cooking. Not even any lights on.

Setting her bag and keys down quietly, she slipped out of her heels and proceeded quietly into the rest of the house, looking for her husband.

Had he fallen asleep?

Or God forbid, just fallen? Hurt himself?

Rustling drew her down the hall and toward their office. Nearing the door, she could see that the light was on. Heard papers shuffling. And then, total silence.

She rounded the corner of the doorway, mouth open on its way to "hello" with perhaps a "how was your day?" attached, and she stopped. Winston was sitting in his chair, turned sideways at his desk, the bottom drawer open, a green hanging file folder sitting next to the stapler not far from his left biceps. Another folder, mostly empty, sat next to the green one.

She noticed because she recognized them—or rather, the markings on the manila one. It was the one in which he'd kept all of the cards she'd given him, notes she'd written that he'd saved for one reason or another, even a few ticket stubs.

Winston's head was down, chin against his chest, his hands against his skull. Her gaze fell to the box between his feet. She recognized the card on top. She'd given it to him the night they were married, but had actually written the page glued inside the day she'd met him. At fourteen she'd just known.

He'd always been as into her as she was him. He'd brought up marriage at fifteen. Talking about their future as though it was a done deal and they'd always be together.

But it wasn't until their wedding night, when he'd read her card, that he'd admitted to her that he'd known, too. That he'd told his mom, the day he'd met her, that he'd met the girl he was going to marry.

He wasn't moving, just sitting there holding his head, that box at his feet.

Was his head hurting? Was he having some kind of breakdown? Or, dare she hope, a breakthrough?

"Winston?" She spoke softly, not sure how to handle the situation. What was best for him. But leaving him like that wasn't an option.

He sat up instantly, his gaze clear, as sharp as always, the second he looked at her.

"Yeah?"

"Your head…is it hurting?" She glanced at the box again and then wished she hadn't. It sat there, an unspeakable wall between them.

"No. I'm fine."

He was not. He just wasn't. And she couldn't take another one of his empty platitudes. They were keeping them locked in a place that went nowhere. Ever.

Her card was in a box on top of a pile that she knew was everything else she'd given him that he'd kept. Except for maybe the one or two things still causing a slight bulge in the folder on his desk. Because he'd chosen to keep them?

And if so, what were they?

Or just because she'd interrupted before he'd completed his task?

The wedding night card was on top. He'd been holding his head.

That meant something.

Desperate as she was, she couldn't let it go.

"Winston, I saw you. You weren't fine. A fine guy doesn't put his chin to his chest and hold his head. He just doesn't."

He stared at her, silent as always.

"Why won't you talk to me?" She might have fallen on her knees in front of him if not for that box in the way. He was hurting. She knew he was. He had to be.

"I do talk to you."

"You said you'd be honest if I asked a question," she remembered, fighting for their lives now.

"That's right."

"So why were you all bent over, holding your head in your hands?"

"I was trying to think."

The words said nothing. And yet they felt important enough that everything in her slowed. Focused. Was he, contrary to what he was telling everyone, having memory problems?

"About what?"

"How to get us out of this entanglement and get you happy."

He wanted her happy. Relief was like fine wine, making her feel bubbly inside. Her Winston was still there. Caring.

"By entanglement, do you mean the current situation? Where we're having to wait for time to help us heal?"

He shrugged.

Or did he mean entanglement as in marriage? She'd been trying for almost two months to keep his divorce comment at bay. To not let it play with her.

And yet there it was. Front and center.

She couldn't voice it. Wouldn't give whatever evil had a hold of him that much credit. Or let it know how much she was growing to fear it.

"Did you come up with any ideas?" she asked, trying not to stare at that box. And needing to know what he'd been planning to do with his things.

"No," he said, his voice sounding almost deflated. "I'm sorry, Emily. I… The way isn't clear. Or easy."

She did fall to her knees then. Right at his feet. "I think that's the job of the 'giving it time' part of this," she told him. "Sometimes you just have to take it day by day and wait for clarity to present itself. Trust that it will."

Lifting a hand, almost as though he was going to run

it through her hair, he let it fall to the top of the folder on his desk. "Is that what you're doing? Waiting for clarity?"

"I'm trusting, Winston, that's what I'm doing." But even as she said the words, another shard of fear shot through her.

What was she trusting? Him? Them? Two months ago, there wouldn't have been a question. But now… Was she still trusting in them, or really just trusting that clarity would come?

Because if what she was trusting was that answers would become clear, there was no guarantee that those answers would contain any way for them to find each other again.

She still wasn't going to consider divorce. Not unless he just went out and did it without her. But the idea of living the rest of their lives in this endless emotional void…

And with a child coming. Could she, in any fairness, do that?

Thinking of the Winston their folks had been seeing these past weeks, she actually entertained the thought that they could pull it off. Stay together, as things were, and raise a child in a loving environment.

Assuming, of course, that Winston was going to take some ownership of his child—that he'd be willing to put up that facade all the time instead of just on weekends. At the moment that assumption felt kind of like counting on the lottery to pay her bills.

But she was discounting time. And the miracle of unconditional love children brought into the world with them.

She glanced down at the box. "What's up with this stuff?"

He knew she knew what it was. At least there was

still enough understanding between them for her to be certain of that now.

"I was clearing it out of the desk."

Clearing it to where?

"You need more space?" she pushed, though her chest felt heavy with the question.

"Not really. I just…didn't want it there."

"Because you want it somewhere else?"

"Yes."

"Where?"

He watched her and silence grew. She couldn't move. Almost couldn't feel.

"My closet shelf."

The tone of his voice, a look in his eye, something warned her that there was more. But she was so damned relieved that their precious mementos weren't going into the trash—even if they'd been headed there minutes ago—that she nodded and rose.

"I'm going to start dinner," she said, and left him alone with his box.

Chapter Fourteen

He didn't want to be a father. He wouldn't make a good one. The child would inevitably be hurt by his shortcomings. His inability to play. Get excited. Express affection. Feel joy.

It wasn't so much that he'd had an "emotionotomy" as it was that he just no longer trusted nebulous sensations that made it harder to do what had to be done.

Some guys got to be dentists and car mechanics. They did their jobs and went home. Winston was a soldier. He was required to lay his life on the line for the good of his country, and that mind-set wasn't something he could let go. He didn't regret the choices he'd made.

At the same time, he had to learn from them.

Loving meant allowing others to count on you.

And they couldn't count on him. Plain and simple.

No matter how many cards and notes and memories swamped him—and they were definitely swamping him more and more as days turned into weeks and months, some just in little ways, others, like the night he'd woken up hard next to Emily, in more difficult-to-brush-off fashion—they didn't change the facts.

His country could count on him. His loved ones couldn't.

Because loyalty and duty won out over love. Love wasn't the huge, all-encompassing highest power as he and Emily had once believed it to be. It hadn't protected "them."

He'd thought about letting Emily in on some of those inner thoughts—trying to help her understand why things were happening as they were—but every time came back to the same assessment he'd had the first night in her home. She'd think he was just suffering from a form of post-traumatic stress. She'd take his words with a "pat on the head" attitude, telling him that in time his feelings would change.

Meaning, would return to what she thought was normal. His counselor continued to give him some of the same rhetoric. Telling him to give it time. Not to make major life-changing decisions in the first six months after his return.

They didn't get who and what he was—that this was his normal now.

Seeing Emily look at his box the other night, he'd been pretty certain that she'd been right to say that time would bring clarity.

Not his. Hers.

He suspected, most certainly after that box hadn't brought about any hint of the faith she'd once expressed so adamantly in them, that time was already making its delivery.

He just had to hang tight. To stay the course. Stick with the plan.

Which was why, Tuesday night, he sought her out in her office before bedtime. "I just wanted to let you know," he said from the doorway, still dressed in the uniform he'd worn to the base that morning despite having no meetings or appointments. "I won't be going with you to tomorrow's appointment."

The decision, while potentially painful to her, was the right one. Building castles in the sand, ones that would be washed away with the tide, was far more damaging in the long run.

Hardly glancing up from her computer, she nodded. "I already figured as much," was all she said. And then, "I'll be ready for bed in about ten. I'm just finishing up a report for Steve to present in the morning."

Surprised at the ease with which he'd pulled that off, most particularly after pondering on it so acutely over the past many hours, Winston went back to watch a little bit more of the baseball game he'd had on.

In a pair of thick black spandex pants, a cross between leggings and pants sworn to be the new dress pant, and a mid-thigh-length tapered white three-quarter-sleeved blouse, Emily stopped in the kitchen for a cup of tea Wednesday morning before heading off to her appointment. Routine usually meant that she showered first and left the house while Winston got ready every morning. She had clients and early meetings, and LA traffic to deal with.

But the clinic didn't open until eight. And it was a five-minute drive. With traffic.

Winston, in his usual khakis and tie, came walking down the hall toward her ten minutes before she had to go. Somehow she'd figured he'd stay in either the bedroom or the office until she left.

"I've changed my mind," he announced. "I'm opting to accompany you to the appointment. In separate cars. I can head straight to the base from there and you can head on to LA as you were planning."

She stared at him. Really needing to figure him out. More than the sex, even the conversation, she missed the way she knew Winston, could tell where he was coming from, how he meant his words, just by watching his face.

"If you're doing this out of guilt, don't," she told him, still sitting at the table, taking a sip of her tea. "I'm truly fine going alone."

A lot of women, even those with husbands who were fully engaged in all ways, went to doctor's appointments alone. "I'll have a video of the sonogram if you want to see it," she added, figuring the mention would send him on his way.

It should have. Every single mention of anything to do with any baby details had had that effect on him so far.

"I'd like to come, Emily. Unless you've changed your mind about wanting me there."

What was he doing to her?

"Of course I haven't." She stood, grabbed her purse and keys, going back to get the cup of tea she'd forgotten and almost left sitting on the table, emptying it and putting it in the dishwasher. Chamomile tea. To calm and soothe. Just in case it really worked. "You ready?"

She led the way out the door, to the clinic and then to the examining room the nurse indicated. Watching for Christine, she wasn't sure if she was relieved or disappointed that the managing director was nowhere to be seen. Not sure if she wanted to introduce the whole Winston being there thing with her or not.

It didn't mean what it looked like—didn't indicate that he was on board.

Or did it?

She lay down as instructed by the technician. Lifted her shirt up to just below her breasts. Tried not to squirm when the cold liquid was squirted on her belly. And to keep an eye on Winston, just to convince herself that she wasn't dreaming and he was really there.

As their love would have demanded.

Their longtime dream might be coming true in unforeseen ways, with god-awful detours, but it really was happening.

She and Winston were having their first ultrasound, to get the first look of their first child.

The monitor sliding across her stomach brought her back to the room, the reality of a screen that would show the truth of what was inside her.

Not a dream.

But a healthy fetus? Suddenly nervous as hell, she stared at the screen, with intermittent glances at the technician. Winston, who'd declined the seat he'd been offered, stood between the technician and the door, meaning, once the test began, she could no longer see him.

She could sure hear him, though. The man had so many questions, and asked them with such swiftness, one after the other, that she didn't have time to worry about what the screen might be showing them.

Bone measurements were taken. Circumferences, too.

"And the heartbeat?" Winston actually seemed to be directing the test, though she knew that wasn't true.

The monitor on her belly lifted, settled, moved, lifted, settled again. "There."

What there? She saw nothing different about the blurs of black and white, shadow and light, she'd been staring at all along. And then she heard it. The faint thumping. When the technician reached over, turned a button, it grew louder. Much louder.

"It's so fast," she said, frowning up from her supine position.

"It's supposed to be," Winston's voice came more strongly to her than the medical professional's who was right beside her. Not because it was louder. It was just what she heard.

"Babies' heart rates are faster than ours," the technician clarified, and then asked, over her shoulder, to Winston, "You a doctor of some kind?"

"No. I'm a soldier."

"I have to hand it to you, then. You're probably the most knowledgeable first-time dad I've ever had."

"I did some reading."

He had? When?

Could the technician tell that Emily's heart rate had just increased? Would that be sounding on the screen next?

"Okay, let's see if we can get this little one to move enough for us to tell whether we've got a boy or a girl..."

Emily stared at the screen off to her right, her heart searching for Winston. Wanting to hold his hand. The monitor on her stomach moved, lifted, pushed, slid, lifted. Until finally, the technician sighed. "Looks like you've got yourselves a stubborn one," she said. "I've taken screenshots that I'll share with my colleague, but I can't get this little one to move enough to give us a clear look."

She glanced over her shoulder at Winston. "Do you have a preference?" she asked him. "A boy or a girl?"

"No."

"How about you?" She looked at Emily, smiling.

She'd been kind of thinking, when she'd first inseminated, that she'd have a boy, someone to take after his father. But now… "Nope. I just want a healthy baby."

And a loving home in which to raise it.

"Well, you've got that," she said, turning things off and wiping the gel from Emily's belly. She gave them a couple of instructions—where to collect the video the clinic would be providing to them, who to see on their way out. Emily wasn't seeing the doctor that day, so they were done.

She paused in the doorway as Emily sat up and started to right her shirt. "Your baby's a lucky one, to have a father as dedicated as you."

"I'm only here to make certain that I know the parameters of Emily's pregnancy so that I can plan for any possible eventualities," he said.

If Emily's entire emotional being hadn't just dropped from the words alone, they would have when she saw the shocked look that crossed the technician's face before the twentysomething hightailed it out of there.

Wow. After they'd just seen their baby move. Heard their baby's heartbeat…

Winston hadn't lost his memory, like she'd momentarily feared in their office the other night. No, he seemed to have lost something far more critical. His heart.

He had to find a way to factor the rapid *thadump, thadump, thadump* of a minuscule cardiac organ into his mission. He'd heard the indisputable fact.

Had caught himself grinning for a second there.

Grinning. Him, a man who'd lived in the middle of bloody carnage, had been…moved. He didn't know what to make of that, either.

How did an emotionally aware guy like himself, one who knew that the illusion of love was as make-believe as Santa Claus, at least where his own capabilities were concerned, get moved by shadows on a screen?

Probably the same way that guy stripped his dead comrade, traded uniforms with him and walked up to the enemy asking to be one of them. You dealt with it by processing the situation and doing what you had to do.

Clearly, when it came to Emily's child, he was going to have to do something.

Keeping in mind that he couldn't be the husband she needed, or the father his child needed. That if she knew the complete truth, she'd know that he'd made their only-each-other-as-lovers-for-our-whole-lives thing impossible. The ultimate proof that their love hadn't been strong enough to save them.

He was still hoping to get them out of the past and into a future where he could do his job and she could have a happy life, without completely obliterating her belief in love and happily-ever-after. She was young. Could still have that dream with someone else. He didn't ever want her to know the full extent of what he'd done.

She was on a need-to-know basis, and she didn't need to know.

He called her on the way home from the base late Wednesday afternoon. They hadn't spoken since parting ways with a quick goodbye in the clinic parking lot that morning. He'd worked out for a couple of hours, driven out to Coronado to watch SEAL training, and then stopped in to chat with the counselor who still wasn't giving him anything good to work with.

Emily's phone hit the fifth ring before she picked up.

"You on your way home?" he asked her straight off.

"Not yet. I'm getting ready to leave shortly."

"I was thinking maybe we'd have dinner out." He named a fine dining place he'd seen on a cliff overlooking the ocean just a few miles from her house. It was new since he'd left Marie Cove for ground training.

"Why?" Her suspicious tone wasn't all bad. It indicated to him that she was progressing as the plan required. As he'd known she would.

Realizing that he wasn't the man who'd married her.

He didn't have to like the job. He just had to get it done.

"I want to," he told her. It was true. He also needed to speak with her with the buffer of others around them who'd necessitate remaining focused on fact, not feeling. Even Emily didn't get emotionally deep out in public. "I've never been there," he added into her silence. "I'm curious about it."

He was doing an awful lot of explaining for a simple suggestion. Noted.

"I've never been, either, and…okay, yes, I'd like to go with you."

She'd never been. Shouldn't matter to him one way or the other. He was bothered that it seemed to matter. That he was pleased.

He wanted a planning session, not memory-building here.

Goal in mind, he headed back to the house to wait for her.

Chapter Fifteen

"We need to talk." They hadn't even had their salads yet. Emily had warned herself not to read anything into the surprising dinner invitation. Still she hadn't been able to stop hoping that it could be a celebration of having heard their baby's heartbeat for the first time that morning.

But "we need to talk"? Everyone knew nothing good came out of that one.

She hadn't bothered changing from the black pants and white blouse she'd worn to work, though he'd offered to wait while she changed. Hadn't let herself create any moments to remember, sitting in his car as he drove to the restaurant she'd told herself she'd never visit without him. "Can we wait until after dinner?" she asked. They'd ordered. Their food was being prepared. Filet mignon for both of them. Because…maybe she had been trying to have a bit of a celebration. Something they'd look back on in the future as a good moment during a difficult time. Something to put in the baby book.

"I need to eat," she said, not caring if she was pulling the baby card. She wasn't going to suddenly fall ill without a meal. And she could have a salad at home. Enough to sustain her and the baby until morning. But she wanted this dinner, here with him, even if it didn't mean what she'd hoped it would.

With a nod, he pulled his napkin from the table and put it over his khakis. Used to be Winston made a point to never wear his uniform anywhere personal. It had been a clear distinction for him.

There was a message in there for her. She'd been getting it. Slowly but surely.

Because they had to fill the silence, or they might as well be having "the talk," she rambled on a bit about her day. A new client she'd been courting for months had just signed. She asked Winston about his workouts. In detail. She used to know how much weight he was pressing. How many miles he ran. The ease with which he shared the answers to her questions had her wondering if maybe she was the one who'd been at the root of the distance between them. At least somewhat. She'd been told to give him time. Which she'd taken to mean to leave him alone, not question him for fear of pushing him into a corner.

Maybe all she'd needed to do was show interest in the little things? Like she used to do?

Their steaks were delivered, cooked to perfection. The view of lights bobbing far out in the darkness beyond the window, the dimly lit room, cloth table covers and well-dressed patrons were all perfection. She wanted to remember every detail. In honor of a healthy heartbeat. And sharing it with Winston.

"This is so good," he said, his eyes alight with a familiar look of appreciation as, fork and steak knife in hand, he went in for another bite.

"Might be the best steak I've ever had," she agreed, smiling at him.

He smiled back and in that second, her whole world was perfect.

She wasn't drinking coffee, but ordered a cup of chamomile tea while Winston drank his after-dinner espresso. Happy just to sit at that table, with that man and their baby growing inside her. The type of moment they'd promised each other when they were fifteen-year-old kids.

Reality sat upon them as well. She didn't ignore that there were struggles in their immediate sphere, but knew that she had to take strength where she could.

Glancing at her husband over the candle in the middle of their table, she wanted to tell him she loved him. Something she hadn't said to him since the first day he'd been back. He hadn't been open to such a declaration.

She had to believe that in time, he would be.

"You need to talk?" She prompted what she'd been sitting there dreading. If it had to happen, better for it to take place now, while she had the strength to know that she could deal with whatever it was. That she could get them through it.

"Yes." Leaning back in his chair, he looked at her like there was nothing else in the room. Not sexually, just like she was all that was there. Her heart skidded, thudded. She reached for the chamomile. Took a hot sip. Felt it go down.

"I need to solidify my role in relation to the child."

Solidify his role? She almost dropped her cup of tea. He wanted a role! Oh God, the heartbeat that morning had worked! Winston was beginning to feel the reality of being a father. To the point that he had to solidify his role!

Telling herself to calm down, to understand that the current Winston wasn't going to be comfortable with a rush of emotion, she held her cup with both hands and nodded.

"I will, of course, provide financial support. That's a given."

Money was the furthest thing from her mind. Not even at the bottom of the worry list. Clearly it was important to him, though, which made it important to her, too. She nodded again. Waiting. He had things to say. She wanted to hear them.

"I need to know all the facts," he told her next. "No matter what happens with you and me, I need to know everything pertaining to the child. Every step of the way. It's the only way to prepare for eventualities."

No matter what happens with you and me.

Calm down, she told herself as a flood of panic surfaced. This was nothing new…

"Of course you'll know," she said, tending to his immediate concern.

"You've been completely silent about the child, lately."

Back to her earlier thought…giving him his space maybe hadn't been the best way to go. She'd talked it over with the counselor—they'd had several phone sessions—and she'd agreed that it was best to let Winston set their pace.

"I didn't think you wanted to know about it." The urge to touch him was so strong, it hurt not to be able to do so.

"I didn't."

Oh. Well, then…

"Now I see the necessity."

Okay. So…that was progress. Time doing its thing. The whole situation was bizarre beyond words, heartbreaking to watch the love of her life struggle so much to reacquaint himself with life. With himself.

And yet…she was so incredibly grateful that they'd been given this chance.

"I'm totally good with that," she told him.

"Okay. So how did you feel today?"

"Fine."

"Your appetite is normal."

"Yep."

"Good."

Reaching out a hand to cover his, she said, "I promise, Winston, from now on I'll tell you everything as it happens."

He was scared. Of losing her. Or the baby. He'd lost so much. Watched his comrades be brutally murdered in front of him, and who knew what else he'd seen during those two years he'd spent living with the enemy. With clarity came a rush of love. And enough strength to move mountains.

He'd made it back to her. Their connection was that strong.

"We'll get through this, Win," she said softly.

Pulling his hand from hers, he nodded and asked for their check.

* * *

"So let me get this straight. You and Emily have been living together, in the home you purchased together, sleeping in the same bed for over two months. You're having a baby! You're reaching understandings. And you still plan to divorce her."

"Yes." Sitting on that blue tweed couch, Winston held Dr. Adamson's gaze and nodded. As strict as she looked in those dark-rimmed reading glasses, with her dress whites and big desk, she just didn't faze him. He was there because he had to be.

Following orders.

He'd made a mistake in telling her about the baby. But with hearing the heartbeat two days before, and then dinner with Emily, he'd figured he should report in, lest she think he was trying to hide things. Or be duplicitous.

"Why?"

It took him a second to get back to their conversation, to know she was referring to the divorce.

"I'm not the man she married."

"So?" Elbows on her desk, she removed her glasses. "She's not likely the woman you married, either. People change."

"I broke our marriage vows."

Dr. Adamson knew the whole story. She'd had a report from his superiors, he was sure, and he'd told her, too.

"So Emily wants the divorce? Because you were unfaithful to her?"

"She doesn't know."

"Oh, so you're just deciding for her that she'd want a divorce because of it?"

If he never heard the woman say "so" again, he'd be quite fine with that.

"I'm saying that *I* want the divorce."

"Why?"

"Because it's the right thing to do."

"Why?"

"Because I'm not who I thought I was. And knowing what I know now, I know I shouldn't be married."

Which made it sound all about him and it wasn't like that.

"I know Emily," he said, sitting forward, his hands clasped together. "I know what she brings to a relationship. And I know what she looks for in one, too. I know what she needs to be happy. I can't give her that. This isn't just a phase I'm going through here, Doctor. This is a well-thought-out, clear choice based on facts.

"They say hard times define you, and I've found that to be true. Before Afghanistan, I believed what I believed. I now know that I wasn't the man I believed myself to be. I'm someone else. Capable of different things. Good things, still, but different. I also know that if I don't divorce Emily, she will stay tied to me for life. That's her. And if she does that, she'll never be happy. I cannot allow myself to rob her of her happiness, to live every day of my life knowing that I'm preventing her from fully living hers, that I'm responsible for her unhappiness."

"These things about you that aren't what you thought… what are you capable of now?"

"Duty, loyalty and protection. Those are the things that have always been there."

"All good husbandly character traits."

The woman couldn't force him to stay married. Even admirals divorced now and then. He wasn't going to engage further on the subject.

"So, Petty Officer Hannigan…tell me what your version of the future with you and Emily and your baby looks like."

In the first place, it was Emily's baby. He didn't choose it. The man who'd made the choice to have a child with her had died in the desert.

The child…biologically was his. He'd take full responsibility for that.

That wasn't what she'd asked. And the brunette barracuda would sit there and stare at him for the last half of their hour, without a word, if he didn't answer her question.

He knew this from experience. One he preferred not to repeat.

The future. Other than Emily apart from him and happy, and him in the naval police, being financially responsible for the child, he hadn't given it a lot of thought.

She was asking beyond his end goal.

He glanced at the clock. Twenty-nine minutes left on his hour.

Then twenty-five. Twenty.

"I hope we'll be on friendly terms," he nearly blurted. So unlike him, that awkward delivery. "I'm supposing we'll be in contact regarding the child. Frequent contact. I'd prefer that to be between the two of us, and I'd think she would like that, too. So, yeah, friendly. Easy. Pick up the phone and call without having to think about it. Or worrying that there'd be tension on the other end."

"And this friendliness…would that only encompass the child? Or could she call you if, say, she had a bad day at work and just needed to tell someone who'd understand?"

"Of course she could. She'd know that."

"What about if there was a death in her family? Could she call you then?"

Was the woman deliberately trying to get his goat?

"She could call me any time she damn well pleases, day or night, about anything she wants to talk about," he said, to make his meaning clear and end the ludicrous line of questioning.

Adamson nodded, her chin pursed in that way that set him on edge. Like Mrs. Kelly, the English teacher he and Emily had had in tenth grade. The thought had him wishing for a second that Emily was there, seeing what he was seeing, because she'd look at him and they'd both laugh.

Except that if he was still the guy who laughed with Emily, he wouldn't be here with Adamson.

"Why haven't you told Emily about the woman in the desert?"

"Because it would hurt her needlessly. She can see enough change in me to end the marriage without bringing that into it. I already feel her pulling away. Where's the harm in letting her go of her own accord, because it's what she wants, without forever bludgeoning her belief in love everlasting? Let her blame it on war and leave the rest out of it."

"You're sure you aren't holding back so she won't hate you?"

"I am absolutely positive about that one. I do not want to hurt her unnecessarily, and that's the only reason I'm not telling her."

Adamson glanced out the window, then back at him and stood. "I think we're done here for the day." They still had eleven minutes. "You're a good man, Petty Officer Hannigan."

Winston had no idea what to make of that.

Chapter Sixteen

Emily drove home Friday night, still energized by Wednesday's after-dinner conversation with Winston. She wasn't going to just sit back and wait for him to come to her.

He'd expressed interest in the baby. More than that. He'd insisted on being a day-to-day, minute-to-minute part of things.

So what if his delivery had been odd. His word choices and body language standoffish. He was there. It was a key she'd been missing. He was there. He was asking.

He was trying to find his way back to her. He needed her to lead the way. She got it now.

She had to engage him.

"Now that we're having weekends to ourselves, I thought we'd start on the nursery tomorrow," she said as they worked together in the kitchen that night, chopping on separate counters while they prepared the stir-fry they'd decided on for dinner.

She was doing all of the grocery shopping, just as she had through all of their years of living together, and cooking together was just as it had always been, too. The activity was part of life. Normal life. Great life.

She chopped onion. He did the peppers and leftover grilled chicken breasts.

"The nursery."

"We'll need to turn the spare bedroom into a nursery," she explained. "Obviously we can't give up the office."

She reminded herself that his silence then didn't mean what it would have meant two years before—that he wasn't on board.

"Where will guests stay when they come to visit?"

"For now, we can keep the double bed set up in there against one wall. Maybe the baby can use it later. We can put a pack-and-play in our room, for the first few months, and keep it afterward, packed away, for the baby to use when we have guests."

"You plan to sleep in the same room as the child for the first few months?"

He didn't like the idea? She could reconsider. But... "I figured with breastfeeding, it would just be easier. We've already got Grandma's rocker in the corner." She could move that to the nursery, though.

The onions were ready. He'd stopped chopping.

"Emily..."

His look was firm. "Yeah?" She looked right back.

"This is important to you?"

It should be important to him, too. She had to believe it would be. "Yes."

"Then I'll help you."

She didn't want his "help." She wanted his involvement, his input. She wanted him to care.

She was being a selfish twit.

He was there.

And that was enough.

Chauffeuring Emily around on Saturday wasn't such a bad deal. Time was passing, bringing him closer to the culmination of the plan, and he wasn't forced to spend full days alone with her in the intimacy of her home.

The whole intimacy thing in general… His body hadn't changed as much as the rest of him had. It wanted to sink itself inside the woman who'd first shown it carnal delights. The only woman it was ever supposed to know.

That night she'd come on to him, when he'd willed himself not to respond, he'd been fairly certain that his body was as enlightened as he was.

A miscalculation on his part.

Following her around in stores, lifting boxes into carts, and then, after paying for them, into the trunk of his car, unloading them, fitting pieces into proper places—it all fit his parameters.

"We really need some paint on these walls," Emily said as he finished putting the crib together without mentioning at all that it seemed a bit premature to build a bed for someone who wouldn't be there for months and months. "I just think we should wait until we know if it's a boy or a girl before we do that," she added. The same thing she'd said when she looked at, and then passed by, sheets and other crib paraphernalia that afternoon.

She was standing there in a short black T-shirt dress, her long legs tanned and perfect as they'd always been, her stomach still looking the same to him.

The same being…rather delicious. And her breasts… He knew them up close and personal and kept picturing the view from the night he'd walked in on her looking at herself in the mirror.

It occurred to him then that painting would be a good activity for the next day. And getting it all done would free him up to be gone as soon as Time convinced Emily that she wanted a divorce.

"There was that one design," he said, willing his body to stay down while sharing that suddenly-too-intimate space with her. "A version of it everywhere," he added, and took a breath as she frowned, watching him like she was concerned.

He didn't need her concern.

"The jungle animals, in shades of green and yellow." The way became clear to him, as it always did. "You could do the walls in those colors, and buy that motif for everything else. It would work for either gender. We can paint tomorrow."

There. He got to the goal. Painting. The next day. So it would be done.

So he'd be busy all day.

So, so, so. Just like Adamson.

What did so have to do with anything?

And when would Time get its butt in gear and get this job done?

He wanted jungle animals. Green and yellow! Lying in bed that night, Emily smiled into the darkness. More and more he was showing himself to her. Oddly, yes. Not like Winston used to. But he was emerging.

She'd been thinking more of pastel rainbows, with an emphasis on blue or pink depending on whether they were having a girl or a boy, but she'd take puce gorillas if it was what Winston wanted.

He wanted *them*.

That was all that mattered.

Which was what she kept telling herself the next day as he acted more like hired help than the man of the house. Her husband. Or the father of her child.

He'd suggested the motif. The colors. And then had stood back and refused to take part in any of the actual choices. And back home, with plastic covering the carpet, he had waited for her to make all of the decisions in terms of what walls were green, which were yellow—she ended up with three a pale yellow and one a bolder green, and then when she wondered about the trim, she had had to decide that, too. She wanted to change it up, do some in green and some in yellow, but hadn't been sure. He gave her nothing.

She figured she'd make the decision when they got to that stage in the painting.

"We need to tell our parents about the baby," she said as they began rolling paint on opposite sides of the room.

He didn't respond. Because he wasn't ready to deal with grandparents? Or just because mute seemed to be his volume of choice these days?

"They're going to know the next time they visit," she said, pointing out the obvious. Besides the new decor for what used to be their spare room, her stomach was already starting to paunch a tiny bit. Her mother would wonder about that.

"That might not be for a while."

True. After the initial flurry of visits, things were settling back down. Before Afghanistan they'd go three months without visits. Everyone was busy, had their own lives. They talked often and that was sufficient.

Painting continued silently, save for the music she'd

put on, a streaming station that played songs from their high school days.

"I want to go this week to have the NIPT test," she offered twenty minutes later. He'd said he wanted to know everything.

"That was the one to determine Down syndrome," he said.

Among other things.

"The child's bone measurements didn't indicate a need."

So he *had* paid attention. In the olden days he'd have talked to her about everything he was thinking. Noticing. Wondering about. So this was a new day. What mattered was that he was there. And he cared.

"The test also tells you the sex of the baby," she told him. "I really want to know. And I think it would be cool to know before we tell the parents, too, so we can give it to them all at once."

She was going to tell Steve in the morning—just so they could plan maternity time for her into the ad campaigns they were developing. Her clients weren't going to feel a blip. She was determined about that. She could work from home as she needed to. And hopefully Steve would step up for the rest.

She'd made him a boatload of money.

And Winston hadn't said a word, which put her on the defensive.

"You said you wanted to be kept apprised of every detail."

"I do."

"I'm going to call the clinic on Monday. I'll let you know when I get the results."

"Thank you."

Thank you? Seriously? Emily turned. Winston was up on a ladder, brush-painting the strip of wall where it met the ceiling, slowly, meticulously, perfectly.

God how she loved him.

And please, God, let it be that he still loved her, too.

Ocean. Air. Sand. Winston didn't know about a God, but he sucked in his surroundings with every breath as he ran on the beach on Coronado Island the following Thursday afternoon. Another week gone. Once time was up he was going to have to push things with Emily. He needed time to get a place to live and settle in before his six months were up.

The thought of being back to work, of strapping on a gun every single day, revved him up enough to add speed to the last of his ten-mile stint. There'd be training first, of course. A nine-week stretch in San Antonio.

Bring it on.

Passing a woman with a little kid, maybe two or three years old, digging in the sand, he thought of Emily. And refused to dwell. They'd remain friends. She'd already agreed to keep him apprised of every aspect of the child's life. Beyond that, any focus on her would be misplaced.

A quarter of a mile later, he was a full scenario deep in imagining her with her baby in the sand. Teaching it to be brave—and safe, at the same time. Encouraging it to explore, to try. And be aware of the sand crabs.

His wrist vibrated, startling him for the second it took him to remember the smartwatch he'd purchased earlier in the week, allowing him to get information even when he was without his phone.

When you were responsible for a woman who was having a child, you had to be ready at any moment for any eventuality. That was the conclusion he'd finally drawn when faced with all of the various things that could happen to a woman, or the child, during gestation.

Glancing at the dial, he saw the call was from her and skidded to an immediate stop. Maybe that nine weeks in San Antonio should wait until after the child was born.

"Hello?" Feeling like an idiot, standing there at the ocean, waves rolling in, talking to his wrist like some damned James Bond wannabe.

"I just wanted to let you know that I got the test results."

"Negative for Down syndrome?" he asked. And then repeated the question for each of the other chromosomal abnormalities for which the NIPT tested, confirming that all were negative.

"We're having a boy, Winston!"

The news slammed him down to his butt in the sand.

She was having a son. Giving Winston a son. A daughter would have been spectacular, too, in an entirely different way. But now, right when Winston needed something to which he could bond, they'd been blessed with a brand-new baby boy. She was back to really believing that the universe was helping them.

He knew what it felt like to be a boy. She didn't. He'd have definite input she wouldn't have. They could talk about Winston taking their son fishing—something Winston and his dad had done together, and something Emily hated. And ball games. He liked them. She, not so much.

Maybe their little guy wouldn't like any of that, either. But Winston could take him. And see.

Little guy.

She was home before he was, had homemade stroganoff ready to serve by the time he walked in the door.

In gym shorts and a sweatshirt. Sweaty. A mess.

And such a hot hunk she got all warm and mushy down below.

"I need to shower," he said, barely looking at her as he walked through the kitchen.

She didn't care. Was grinning so big her face muscles cramped. He'd come home in personal clothes. Not his uniform.

The change came about the day he'd found out he was having a son. It could be a coincidence. She didn't think so. The universe was looking out for them. She only had to trust.

Still jittery with excitement, Emily set the table, filled plates and sat down across from Winston.

"Have you thought of any names?" she asked as she took her first bite of noodles, starving more than usual that night.

She'd already put on a couple of pounds. If she wasn't careful she was going to become an elephant. A happy one, but still…she had to be healthy if she hoped to keep up with the two guys in her family in years to come.

"Names?" He glanced at her, frowning.

She chose to focus on the jeans and T-shirt he'd donned. A shirt from a vacation they'd taken in Italy several years before. They'd had sex in the Jacuzzi in their suite—the first time they'd done it in the water.

"For the baby," she told him. She'd been playing with ideas all afternoon. Was eager to discuss them with him.

"No." He was tending to his dinner like he hadn't eaten in weeks.

The stroganoff was extra good that night. She'd outdone herself. "I was thinking about Winston James, for you and my dad," she told him. "But if you'd rather have Winston Dane the Second, I'm great with that, too."

He continued to eat.

"What do you think?" she pushed him. Remembering their dinner out on what would always be the night of the heartbeat to her. The night she'd finally understood more of what Winston needed from her. The night she'd been so close to giving up hope and had gained it afresh instead.

"I don't have any thoughts on the matter. Except…"

Getting a little more used to his acerbic ways of dropping his desires into their conversations, she grabbed that "except" like a lifeline. "What?"

"I don't think he should bear my name."

Wow. That was a surprise. He'd always talked about having a little namesake. One for him and one for her. Their other two children would be named for their favorite constellations and mythical characters. Of course, they'd been fifteen when they'd made those decisions, too.

And maybe he was right. Two men in the same home with the same name could become confusing. There'd be the issue of needing a nickname for the baby, something he'd have to be called to distinguish him from his father, meaning he'd never be able to go by his real name.

"What would you like?" she asked.

He shrugged, helped himself to another spoonful of stroganoff. "Anything but Winston," he told her.

Not much for her to go on. But she'd wanted his input. He'd told her what mattered to him.

And what mattered to her was that he was there. And he cared.

Chapter Seventeen

He was going to miss living in the house. Having dinner with Emily. Sleeping with her close. And yet he couldn't wait to be away from the confusing array of challenges that being with her presented.

Mess after mess after mess. Winston did not like messes. Messiness. And found himself surrounded by situations that just were not straightforward.

Names. Nurseries. Colors. Giraffes. Breasts. Bellies. Parents.

Oh, the parents. It would have been much cleaner to tell his parents about the child after he was out of Emily's house, when he was telling them about the divorce, so they'd better understand. Then they'd know that he wasn't the happy expectant father they'd assume him to be. That he wasn't a father at all.

But Emily had had a good point. As soon as someone came to the house, the news would be out. And would spread. Her mom and his were still friends from when they all lived in the same town together. Not best friends. But they'd definitely connect over this one.

So he'd called them. Making certain to do it by himself, toning down the news as a fact, rather than a celebration. Trying to preempt more cacophony.

He'd failed there, too.

He might only be a biological component, as opposed to a real father, but his folks were definitely grandparents. The child was little more than a tiny pooch in Emily's belly. Nothing anyone would notice if they didn't know to look. But that heartbeat sound, in MMS, flew over cell towers from Emily's phone to his parents, and plans had been piling up on his back ever since.

They'd sent outfits. The moms wanted to plan a shower. They talked about Christmas—which was still three months away and long after his divorce would happen. And three months before the child would be born.

Ramifications of that sperm he'd had stored all those years ago were spiraling out of control.

Out of his control.

When Emily suggested heading to bed early on Saturday night to watch some television, he followed right after. They'd made a vow, during those naive teenage years, to always go to bed together. While he was living in her home, he was respecting her rules. But as he climbed in beside her, catching a glimpse of her thigh as he lifted the covers, the mental and physical effort it cost to remain immune was a clear message to him. He couldn't wait much longer to move on.

Winston's hand was on her hip. Instantly alert, Emily lay still in the darkness, hardly daring to breathe, to move her body even that much. In all the weeks since his return he'd never even come close to instigating physical contact with her in bed. Or anyplace else when they were alone.

The only times he reached out to her, made any physical connection at all, had been when their folks were around.

On her side, her back to him, she could feel her nipples hardening.

The hand just lay there, on top of her panties. Her gown had slid up to her waist and with the exception of the panties, the rest of her was bare. Desire flooded her so fiercely she was almost certain he'd know it. Thought about him knowing what that simple touch was doing to her.

As badly as she wanted to roll to her back, to welcome him, to touch him, too, she didn't. The last time she'd tried, the only time either one of them had ever rejected the other, had hurt too badly to risk a replay. It was taking every ounce of her strength, of her faith in him and in them, to keep her head above the particularly rough sea of her emotions these days. Pregnancy hormones were a bitch.

But she was eager and ready for him if he wanted more.

Listening, she couldn't tell by his breathing if he was awake or asleep. He breathed heavier when he was turned on, too.

After several minutes, she was still wide-awake. Even if Winston wasn't aware of what he was doing, wasn't coming on to her, she didn't want to doze off and miss a second of his touch. She missed him so incredibly much. Just that hand…it shored up her strength. Reminding her how truly connected they were. Just his touch on her hip could make her world so excitingly right.

She'd lie there until morning if he chose to…

The hand moved. Steeling herself, she waited for his

touch to be gone, leaving her alone in the dark. No…no, wait… It moved up a little, not away. And then…down a little past where it had started out. Three more times his hand moved across her hip, over the panties to the skin on either side, leaving tingles in its wake.

On the next pass, his hand went farther down her leg, and then farther up her side, beneath her nightie. She worried about her elbow getting in the way, yet feared moving. If he thought she was asleep, if he was trying to wake her in the way he'd woken her so many times in the past, she didn't want him to know he'd succeeded. Not yet.

She had no way of knowing if he'd continue to love on her once she awoke. Or if her consciousness would send him back into the lonely world he inhabited these days.

He was welcome to her comforts for as long as he wanted them. The rest of the night, if he needed it that way.

His hand veered off course when it reached her elbow. But the barricade didn't stop him as she'd feared. His hand continued upward, on the inner side of her arm, reaching her breast easily, so…confidently…she sucked in a breath. Feared he'd stop at any second.

He didn't stop. His hand covered her breast, nipple in the center of his palm, as though he'd been there the night before, not more than two years ago. Teasing her nipple with his palm as he gently held the rest of her breast, he proceeded to get her good and wet. Just as he'd been doing since they'd been way too young. He knew her body and played it as she'd taught him. Just with that one hand on her breast.

His body was against her back, spooning her, without her being aware of either of them moving. He continued to tantalize her breast…and to push his very hard, very generous sexual part between her thighs. That's when she realized he was still wearing the boxers he put on for bed these days. Part of him had found its way out and nudged her thighs, and she waited to see what he'd do next.

Take off the boxers, or just take her with them? Either way, she planned to get them off him sooner or later. She needed to touch, to see, to taste every part of this man she'd been loving in some fashion since before she was born.

Moaning, she lifted her top thigh, giving him access, and...

A rush of cold air hit her right between the legs. Her breast ached, not in a good way, from the force with which Winston's hand had moved away.

Away?

Thinking that he was taking off his boxers, she rolled over, eager to see whatever the night's shadowy darkness would show her.

She saw the wall. Bringing her gaze in closer...an empty bed.

"Winston?"

He was in the rocker, half bent over, his arms resting across his knees.

"Winston!" she cried, instantly out of bed and on the floor at his feet. She reached for him and when he didn't move, she settled for a hand on his arm.

"What is it, Win? Are you hurt? What's wrong? Should I call 911?"

Flashes of thought sped back and forth across her mind. Heart attack? Something internal down below? Prostate trouble? Had he come too soon? Had a flashback to his time in captivity?

When he didn't move, didn't speak, fear flared so starkly within her, she yelled at him.

"Winston, answer me, dammit." Getting up as she

finished, she added, a bit less fiercely, "I'm going to call an ambulance."

"No."

Unlike her, he didn't raise his voice at all. He raised his head, though, looking her directly in the eye. Glint to glint in the near darkness.

Falling back down in front of him, she put her hands on his knees. "What's going on?"

He just stared at her, his nostrils moving with the force of his breathing. Or emotion. No other tells at all. Nothing.

"Please talk to me, Win. Let me help."

"You want to know how you can help?" He sat there in his T-shirt, still hiding his midsection, holding her captive with a look.

"Of course. Anything. I love you so much, Win. I'll do whatever it takes. Anything." She just couldn't stress it enough.

"Let me out of here," he said.

Of all the things she'd been preparing to hear, that hadn't even been a blip on a radar. "What?" Then her brain caught up. "You need to go for a walk?" she asked. "Or a drive?"

She scooted back, sitting on the floor, her arms on her own raised knees now. "Of course," she said. "I didn't mean to pin you to the chair. I just... Go ahead." With an arm, she motioned to the door.

At some point he was going to have to tell her what was going on. But this moment didn't have to be it—right now wasn't about her.

"No, Emily." He finally sat up, forearms on his knees now, hands clasped. "I need you to let me get the divorce. We're going nowhere."

They'd been about to go somewhere pretty damned spectacular.

Frowning, she replayed his words, trying to understand from a perspective outside the panicked one suddenly invading her entire system.

The intensity of their lovemaking had scared him. That had to be it. And just like when he'd first come home…he'd jumped immediately to divorce. Because he felt threatened.

It was all residual from having been held captive in an enemy camp for two years, not knowing, every single day, if he would make it to nightfall. Not knowing if he'd ever get out.

She couldn't even imagine the horror—and he'd lived it. Every single second of every day. While she'd been right there in their home in Marie Cove. Going to work every day. And safely to bed on their mattress in their room.

"We've made a lot of progress, Win," she said softly, hating that she'd yelled at him. And scared to death that she didn't have the right words for him then. It was four in the morning. It wasn't like she could call someone. "You chose the nursery design," she reminded him, trying desperately to think back over all of the things that had happened to give her hope. "You came to the ultrasound," she said. "You're joining in on every aspect of our lives. It has to be because they mean something to you." She told him what she'd been telling herself. "You're here, you care. That's all that matters. The rest will come. You just need to give it more ti—"

"No." He stood, but it wasn't the force of the movement that had her eyeing him in shock. It was the tone of voice. Loud. Stern. So completely lacking in any tenderness at all that she didn't even recognize it as Winston.

"No more time, Em," he said softly.

Her entire being recognized that tone. And the way

he said her name. She hadn't heard it since the morning he left for ground training. Tears in her eyes, she turned, still on the floor, to face him where he'd dropped to sit on the edge of his side of the bed.

"Time's what it takes, Win," she said back, equally soft, the words filled with all of the love she had bottled up inside. "Time will take care of *us*."

He knew that. Somewhere inside him, he *knew* that.

"I thought time would do it, too, but it hasn't. It isn't," he said to her.

Jumping off the floor, Emily sat beside him, her hip pressing up against his. She took his hand and looked at him until he looked back, their lips close enough for a kiss.

"I'm not going to give up, Winston. Not tonight. Not tomorrow. Not ever."

Their wedding vows. She hadn't sat down to say them. They'd just come to her. They'd promised each other, among other things, that nothing would ever separate *them*. He was a sailor. They'd been facing a life of him being gone for long stretches on ship. But no matter where he was, in what part of the world or for how long, nothing would separate *them*. They'd promised.

"I gave up, Em." He was all Winston now. The man she knew. And loved with every fiber of her being. It was a miracle, the way the stranger in their midst had simply vanished.

"I know this is hard for you—I know you've been through hell. You were facing imminent death every second of every day," she told him. "You'd seen guys you'd cared about be blown up right in front of you. But you didn't die, Win. And you didn't give up. You'd never have made it back if you had. But you *did* make it back. Just like you promised. I can't tell you why, in a practical, technical sense, your life was spared, but what I know for certain is that when it *was* spared, you kept yourself alive. You came back to us. And the entire two years you were gone, I could feel you. People would tell me you were dead. Your commander, he said you'd died, but that they couldn't find your body...but I didn't believe it, Win. Because I could still feel you. Just like, somewhere deep inside you, you could feel me. It sounds nuts, but it's always been that way with us, you know that. Even if you can't feel it right now, you must remember..."

"I remember."

Oh God, the miracle of this night. She couldn't help the tears that flooded her eyes, the way her hands shook as she held on to him.

"You'll feel it again, Win. I'm as sure of that as I am that you kept yourself alive for us, and that I believed you were alive the whole time. It's who we are. It's what we do. What we've always done..."

She couldn't stop saying it. The truth was in her core and there was no silencing it anymore. She was fighting for them, and she'd never stop fighting...

"I married a woman in the Afghan desert, Em. I lived with her. I slept with her."

The words knocked Emily's heart unconscious.

And she couldn't fight.

Chapter Eighteen

Winston moved out a couple of hours later. He didn't take much with him. Just the duffel he'd come in with. A few extra toiletries he'd purchased in the interim. And some clothes. Until their lawyers could put paperwork together, until he knew where he stood with San Antonio and finances, he'd be staying at the barracks.

He'd asked if she minded keeping his things at the house for a while longer.

She'd said the house belonged to both of them and seeing that his things had been there for the past two years, she didn't think another few months would matter. Or something to that effect.

She hadn't asked a thing about Afsoon. Not even her name. She'd been in shock. And then she'd just shut down on him.

He'd known what it would do to her—telling her. Hadn't meant to do so.

But he'd almost made love with her in his sleep.

No way could he do that to her—make love to her with her thinking he was what he'd always been—that he'd been inside no woman but her.

He'd been tested—he wasn't carrying anything. But with him and Emily, their fidelity to each other hadn't been one damned thing to do with health.

And their relationship had been everything about truth. Some guys could have a thing on the side—maybe just once in a marriage, even, a true mistake—and say nothing. He wasn't that guy.

And he could no longer trust himself to live with Emily and not make love to her. His time was up.

He picked up a six-pack of beer on the way to the base that morning. And once he was settled in the furnished one-bedroom unit he'd been assigned, sheets and towels included, he popped the top on the first bottle. He could put them away with the best of them. Just hadn't done so in a long time.

He did that Sunday. He finished off the six-pack. Thought about taking a walk for more, but ended up lying on the bed, watching football. One game. Then two. On to the night game. He couldn't say who was playing, much less who won. Didn't give a rat's ass about who ran for how many yards, how many completed passes he saw, or who was out with injuries.

He cared about Emily.

When it started to get dark, he called her.

"Hello?"

He hadn't really expected that she'd pick up. "How are you?"

"Fine."

"I'm sorry, Em. So sorry."

"Yeah, me, too."

"What did you do today?"

"Bought a wardrobe of clothes for Tristan Dane, three different sizes, sheets and little hoodie towels, disposable diapers and a year's worth of baby wipes."

He'd asked.

"Tristan Dane?" She was naming the child after him? Even then?

"I know you didn't want him to have your first name, but he's part of you and a boy needs to feel like he's part of his father. Since I can't guarantee that you'll have an active role in his life, I at least want him to know he was important enough to you to carry part of your name."

Lying on his bed, only the television's glow for light, he wished he had more beer. "You decided all that today?"

"Most of it. I'd already decided on the name."

And she hadn't changed her mind. For the child's sake.

He'd muted the television, but the game was back on, following the commercial break that had finally pushed him into calling her. It was hard to forget your marriage was over when you were watching an insurance commercial depicting a happy family living a great life.

Maybe if he'd bought some of that particular insurance his unit wouldn't have ended up on the wrong end of enemy fire.

"Why'd you pick up when I called?" he asked, the beer no longer making him sleepy, but still affecting him enough to allow the question to slip through.

"You're Winston. I've picked up every time since the very first time you called me."

He figured it would only be a matter of time until that changed. Because everything did.

She didn't ask him about Afghanistan. About any of it. And since he had nothing that could help her, he rang off.

The next evening, he was right in the same exact place. Lying propped up on pillows on the double bed, a football game on the television. He'd brought another six-pack of beer back to his place, along with a sub, but was only on his second drink.

He'd had a good workout that day, followed by another Coronado beach run. Then a meeting with a group of men and women who were working to keep the United States safe from terrorist attack. He'd had no idea he'd retained so much information during his time in captivity, but was glad he had. At least he was good at the thing he was built to do.

He'd canceled his meeting with Adamson. He'd catch up with her later in the week.

Lobbing the sub bag toward the trash can in a corner of the room, he gave himself two points for making it. And the phone rang.

Emily.

"Hello."

"I need to know, Winston."

"Know what?"

"All of it. Who is she? Did you know her before you were captured? How long have you been...*married*...?" Sounded like she gritted her teeth on the last word. "Where is she now? Have you been in contact with her since you got back?" Her voice broke then.

Muting the television, he stared at the nondescript beige wall, wishing he'd died that day in the desert, right beside Danny.

"Her name is Afsoon."

"Afsoon." Bitterness mixed with tears. It was a sound he would never forget.

"I told you that I went to the village as a traitor to my country…"

"Posing as one, yes."

The distinction—that she made it even after knowing what he'd done to her, to their marriage—didn't surprise him. Emily was Emily. One in a million.

Which was why, once he'd met her, he'd never cared to seriously look at another woman.

"I told you that they tested me, the first test being that I kill a US soldier and bring them the body, as a sign of my loyalty."

"Yes. Danny. You used Danny's body, dressed in your uniform." Her tone was stronger. And yet…unknown to him. Lacking in whatever made her Emily.

And he wondered, as he watched a quarterback complete a relatively simple pass, if he'd been sounding that way to her all these months.

While she'd stood by him. Still believing.

If only he'd been able to hold himself in check for a little while longer. Just until her belief had been challenged as his had. He'd so badly wanted her to see, to look at him and know that their childhood fantasies had been just that. Then he wouldn't have had to tell her all of this. They could have remained friends more easily that way.

And she wouldn't be sitting home alone so desperately hurting.

He went for a third beer. Uncapped it. Downed half the bottle.

"The remote village I was in was controlled by Taliban sympathizers. Many of their customs… They're hard for anyone raised in Western civilization to understand."

He'd lived among it and still didn't get it. And prolonging things wasn't making this any easier. He just had to tell her.

"Marriages are commonly arranged, with the groom or his family paying the bride's family. I didn't have any way to pay for a bride, but they wanted me to have my own woman. They 'gifted' me with a bride about six months after I'd joined them. I determined that it would blow my cover if I didn't comply."

They'd have known he wasn't truly one of them if he hadn't accepted the gift.

"So you were married, living with her, sleeping with her for a year and a half?"

The pain in her tone burned through him.

"Are you familiar with *bacha posh*?"

Silence followed his question—a nonanswer to her own. And then, "No." Even with just the one word, he could tell she was crying.

All of this misery couldn't be good for the child.

"It's a fairly common and accepted custom in parts of Afghanistan and Pakistan where a family without a boy child raises one of their daughters in that role. She is dressed like a boy, has her hair cut short, and is then allowed in society, to escort her young sisters who have no brother to escort them. She's allowed to attend school with the other boys and to play sports, sometimes, too."

He'd had no idea…until he'd met Afsoon.

"When the girl reaches puberty, however, she's thrust back into the female role."

Emily hadn't made a sound. He could still feel her pain, singeing his nerve endings.

"Afsoon was a bacha posh. She'd grown up going to school with a group of boys training to be soldiers. She'd learned all she could with them, wanting more than anything to be a soldier herself. She had great difficulty settling into a more submissive female role. When it came time to choose a wife for me, her family offered her up for free. By that time I'd already figured out who to listen to, and when and where pertinent conversations took place, and I knew that a deal had been made. Afsoon had offered herself up so she could be a good soldier and keep an eye on me. It gave her a chance to meet with the boys she'd grown up with. To report in. To be one of them, even if just for a few minutes a week."

"Did you love her?"

He understood why she'd asked the question. And hated the foreignness of it at the same time. "No." He'd admired her, though. Respected her.

"But you had sex with her."

Thinking of Emily every single second. He wasn't sure what that made him. He'd done what he'd had to do. And would do it again, given the same circumstances.

"Enough to keep up the pretense, yes."

"Did you have children with her?"

"No." She hadn't wanted his children any more than he'd wanted to give them to her, not that she'd told him so. But they'd both been very obviously careful to make certain it didn't happen, in spite of a lack of easy access to traditional birth control.

"What about her? What happens to her now that you're gone? Won't they suspect she helped you escape?"

"She did help, in a way—though it wasn't her intention. I'd heard her planning with a childhood best friend, a soldier in the village, for the two of them to run off together. There was access to a Jeep that would take them to a convoy they were joining. They decided to set a fire during a village celebration to buy themselves time to get away. I used their diversion as my own chance to get the hell out of there."

"Was it good with her?"

"My leaving? She didn't know."

"The sex, Winston."

"Emily. Don't do this."

"Answer me, dammit. Was it good with her?"

"It was sex, Emily. Men like sex."

"So you liked it."

"No! It was… I got it up, okay, that was it."

"And afterward. Did you hold her close as you fell asleep?"

"No." He hadn't fallen asleep beside her. He'd been lying next to the enemy. His only real sleep had come in the afternoon, when he'd had time alone to pray and study.

"I have to go."

Emily hung up on him before he'd had a chance to tell her, once again, how very sorry he was.

For the next week, visions of Winston in bed with another woman, a dark-haired beauty with lusciously tanned skin, stabbed her again and again, throughout the day, and lying in their bed alone at night, too. The woman was there in Emily's dreams, turning them to nightmares. She found a pair of his underwear left in the laundry he'd sorted before he left, and pictured the other woman washing them by hand.

Not that it would have been the same exact pair, but…

Hands other than her own traveling her husband's body, knowing his touch, his particular scent, the way he moved his body when he was inside you.

She was crushed. Absolutely flat on the ground crushed. She went to work Monday, but not Tuesday. She spent that day, and the next, at home, lying on the couch, watching television, sleeping on the couch during the day because she wasn't getting a whole lot of sleep at night.

After the second day of living like a sloth, she woke up Thursday morning, shook herself off and dressed for work.

The idea of Winston with another woman wasn't such a shock anymore. Acceptance was on its way, she could feel it. The barbs would poke her for the rest of her life; she pretty much accepted that. Anytime she thought of him with her.

But she'd get used to them. Push past them.

And in time, they'd come less frequently, as he was less frequently on her mind.

She just had no idea where she went with the rest of her life without him.

He'd called every day. She hadn't picked up.

He'd broken their most sacred vow. The rest had been flushed away with it.

But she knew, as she drove to work that Thursday, a few days after she'd last spoken with Winston, that she couldn't really blame him for what he'd done. He'd been in a life-or-death situation.

She'd rather he be alive than dead.

But "them." She'd really truly believed in the sacredness. That they were somehow special, protected. That as long as they each believed, neither of them would ever break their vows.

She called Winston on the way home from work Thursday evening, using her car's voice commands. It was almost dark. She'd stayed late getting caught up. Had discussed maternity leave in depth with Steve as well, going through each client on her list. She was going to be a mother. She'd had her time to fall apart, and now she had to continue doing all she could to make the most out of life.

The fourth ring sounded through her speaker system. He wasn't answering.

And then he did.

"Emily? Sorry, I was in the shower. Is everything okay?"

"It's fine. I'm on my way home and just wanted to apologize…for my behavior earlier this week. I'm sorry I didn't pick up when you called. I will do my best to never let that happen again."

She wasn't making forever promises anymore. Ever. They weren't real.

"You have no need to apologize," he told her. "None. This is on me, Em."

"It's life." She gave him the conclusion she'd come to. It happened whether you believed it would or not. "I also want you to know…I don't blame you for what you did. It was the best choice, given the circumstances." She couldn't tell him she was glad he'd slept with another woman. Married her. Lived with her for a year and a half. Her heart was too raw to go that far.

"I'm assuming that the navy, or whoever in the government has the power, has seen that the marriage is legally ended?"

"A lot of Afghan marriages aren't registered with the government, or in an official capacity like ours are. This one was not. And technically, it was Danny she married. And it is believed that I, posing as Danny, am now assumed dead in Afghanistan."

"Do you know if Afsoon got away?"

"She did not. Nor did her soldier friend. They're both dead. From what I'm told it's believed that they killed me in their attempt to get away. I don't know how accurate that source is, though. A contact that we have over there made a trip to the village ostensibly to help rebuild after the fire, but really to see what he could find out, and that's what he got from a kid in the village."

"Wow. That's horrible."

Truly, truly horrible.

So much worse than a husband who slept with someone to save his life.

Worse, even, than finding the love you thought you'd shared, a one-of-a-kind, preordained, protected-by-powers-greater-than-self kind of love, had been nothing but a figment of her imagination.

"I saw that you called," she said as the conversation lagged between them—something that, until Winston's return, had never happened before. "Did you have something you needed to discuss?"

Had he already met with his lawyer? she translated silently.

"Just checking in," he said.

She understood that. Appreciated it. Wasn't at all sure what to do with him now that she knew he hadn't been chosen specifically for her.

Because if he had, by her understanding, he wouldn't have been put in the untenable position of having to sleep with someone else to stay alive.

"Okay, I'm doing well, so how are you doing?"

"Fine. I've sent up a request for naval police training. It's a nine-week stint in San Antonio. And then I'll get my orders."

Even after he'd finished basic and received orders for San Diego, they'd always known he'd most likely be transferred at some point. She just hadn't really given the idea much credence.

They were "them." They'd both grown up in Marie Cove. Loved it there. When his orders had come through to ship out from San Diego, she'd almost taken them as an inevitability. She'd expected them.

So young. And naive.

And now…

"You could be sent anywhere."

"I know."

And if he got the divorce he wanted? Where did that leave Tristan in terms of knowing his father? And where did it leave her, living, perhaps, across the world from her best friend for the rest of her life?

She needed to ask. Wasn't ready for the answer yet.

But there was one thing she had to know. Based on the man she'd gotten to know over the past months. This new Winston—or the one he'd always been and she just hadn't seen—always had a goal in mind. Worked toward the goal.

"What is your goal where you and I are concerned?" she asked him. And then quickly clarified, "Not legally, but in terms of us? How do you see us working out?"

The question was clear in her mind. Coming out, it sounded pretty stupid.

"As friends, Em. Good friends. Always. Our history alone shapes that, doesn't it?"

His answer spoke straight to her heart.

And made her sad, too.

Chapter Nineteen

On Friday, Winston was turned down for master-at-arms "A" school in San Antonio. He was invited to re-apply when his six-month leave was up and he had all the necessary return-to-active-duty signatures.

And the following Monday morning, he received word that he was being offered an early honorable discharge at the convenience of the government, in spite of the fact that he had a full year left on his commission.

Could be in light of his sacrifice. Or perhaps because he'd gone rogue. That wasn't made clear, and Winston didn't ask.

He wasn't required to take the offer.

The commander who met with him suggested that he talk the decision over with his wife.

While he actually wanted to hear what Emily thought, he knew it wasn't fair to treat her like a wife when they were going to be divorcing.

After the divorce, once they were settled into a routine, then he could talk to her about that kind of stuff again.

He went to Adamson instead. He had the appointment. Now he had a reason to go it.

"I'm assuming you had something to do with my being turned down for 'A' school?" he asked as he was taking his usual seat in a corner of the old blue couch.

"No." The infuriating woman folded her hands on her desk and looked at him, calm as ever. "I wasn't consulted," she said.

So it had just been because he was still on leave, not because his therapist had derailed him. For once she'd said something that actually pleased him.

In his good mood, he told her that he'd come clean with Emily. That they'd separated and would be getting a divorce.

And then he talked about "A" school again. He needed a good plan for the rest of his life.

"What about your child?" she asked him.

"Emily and I have already discussed all that," he told her. "I'm taking full responsibility, of course."

"I just meant…being a father is a good life plan…"

Frustrated again, he sat forward, elbows on his knees, ready to push off.

"Fathers have to have careers to pay support," he reminded her.

"I'm just thinking…with you and Emily splitting, and then you being in the navy, with the possibility of being transferred anywhere in the world…you might not get a chance to know your son all that well…"

He was fairly certain he'd already made clear to her that he was only a biological parent in this situation.

Although, as he sat there, all of the reasons why that

had to be didn't come immediately to mind. Or didn't ring as strongly true when he did manage to call them up.

So he didn't believe that love was true. Or that "love of my life" was meant to be taken literally. He didn't believe in Santa Claus, or some great power that watched over them all. He still had a lot of things he could teach the boy. Loyalty, for one. And duty.

How was he going to protect him if he was halfway around the world?

Emily could give the child all of the love Tristan needed.

But Winston still had valid things to offer.

"I got a notice this morning that you've received an offer for early discharge," Adamson said as Winston sat silently contemplating—defensively guarding his thoughts from the woman who'd been trying to make him something he was not from the very beginning.

He'd actually meant to talk to her about the discharge. Since he wasn't talking to Em about it.

"I was planning to re-up when my year is through," he said now. Military life fit him. It spoke to all of his strengths.

"You want to be military police."

"I think I'd be good at it. And enjoy the work."

"So...have you considered civilian law enforcement? You've got the weapons training. If you want to stay with the navy, there's always NCIS. You could request the Los Angeles office and with your record and history, I'm pretty sure you'd be given serious consideration for any special agent openings they might have."

He hadn't seriously considered anything but "A" school. He'd needed a goal to set his mind on, and that had been it.

Was still it.

The navy was his only constant.

"Have you talked any of this over with Emily? I'm assuming, since you said you'd moved out, that she's agreed to the divorce?"

"She knows that what we thought we had doesn't exist."

"But again, have you asked her what she wants? Or just determined what you can't give her?"

"I have my goals," he told her.

"Career goals, yes, but there are other aspects to life. Equally, if not more important, aspects."

Not for him there weren't.

He wasn't getting sucked into happily-ever-after again. Turned out, he wasn't good at it.

"My career is my goal," he restated, because he had to set the woman straight. "No matter what I do…whether it's walking dogs, being a cop or fighting wars, I am always going to be the man who, if faced with danger, will act. I will risk my life to save others. That's what I have to offer. Not a promise that I'll come home. Or even put home first."

"You had a crisis in the desert, Soldier." Adamson's tone was stern, firmer than he'd known her to be, her gaze as direct as any commander under which he'd ever served. "You were forced to turn your back on what mattered most to you personally—your love for your wife—in order to serve your country."

He bristled. Did not need her telling him what he already knew.

"My wife doesn't come first."

"Yes, she does. For you personally, yes, she does. And

that's the entire basis of the crisis you're in and have been in since you made your choice in that desert."

He wasn't in crisis. He was in reality.

"You want to know what I think?" she continued.

"Not really."

"I think that changing identities with Danny like you did—a young man with no wife, no Emily, no soul mate—was what allowed you to do what had to be done. Somehow, in some place in your psyche, you became Danny. Because it's what you had to do to survive. To help others survive. You're one of the strongest men I've ever known, Winston, and I'm not speaking about physical strength here. You've got a mind that's as strong as you are. The things you did, your ability to get out with your sanity intact… I'd go to battle with you anytime."

What the hell? Sitting still, about as uncomfortable as he'd ever been in a professional situation, he stared at her. Was she building him up for some big piece of bad news?

"It's time to let Danny go."

Emily was staring at her belly in the mirror Saturday morning, one day short of two weeks since she'd seen Winston. She was really starting to show. Not enough to require new clothes, but enough that she couldn't wear her tightest outfits anymore. Or button the top of her jeans. Hard to believe the change was suddenly happening.

Running her hand over her belly, she tried to imagine what Tristan was going to look like. Couldn't wait to meet him. She might not be the happiest wife in the world, but she was most definitely one of the happiest mamas. In spite of everything, maybe even because of everything, she wanted her baby more than anything.

Her mom called, wanting to come up to go baby shopping, and she put her off. No one knew Winston had moved out yet and she wasn't ready to tell them.

He'd been calling pretty much every day. Just to check in. The calls were short. Mostly impersonal, if daily calls could be considered that. One of these days the call was going to include talk of lawyers. Settlements.

Every time he hung up without mentioning any of that, she was thankful—and then angry with herself for being thankful. It had to come. She wasn't stupid enough to think otherwise. Wasn't even sure she'd want otherwise.

Their life had been based on childhood farce. At least on her part—she couldn't speak for him. They didn't talk of such intimate things.

But maybe they should.

Picking up the phone she'd just set on the counter after her mother's call, she dialed Winston. Asked him if he had time to get together that day. Any place of his choice.

And so two hours later found her pulling into a parking spot by the Navy Pier in downtown San Diego. He'd suggested lunch at the pier—Top of the Market. More linen tablecloths. Excellent seafood. And views of the bay. Way too nice a place for the conversation she'd envisioned, so she ate too much, talked about the view and assured him she felt perfectly normal and fine. It was good just to see him. If he noticed her thickening stomach in the leggings and long gray T-shirt she'd worn with flip-flops, he didn't say.

But then, she didn't say anything about the black jeans and white button-down shirt he had on, and she definitely noticed them. It had been a long time since she'd seen Winston's backside in black jeans. A long, long time.

Understandable that she'd have the urge to walk slightly behind him to prolong the pleasure.

Even knowing they were divorcing, that she'd never have sex with him again, that sight turned her on. Of course, she'd never made a point of allowing her gaze to settle on another man's ass. Might be that any of them would do the trick. Like a guy looking at breasts.

To test the theory, she checked out several butts on their way out of the restaurant and then as they walked along the pier.

Nothing really struck her.

It could be that there just weren't a lot of great butts walking around that Saturday afternoon. Or any other black jeans.

"I need to ask you something," she said as they walked toward the docks.

Winston pointed to a white bench set off in the grass, under a tree. "You want to sit?"

"Why don't we walk down and look at some of the boats?" she suggested instead.

"I think we should sit. I need to speak with you, too."

She shouldn't have come. Shouldn't have pushed this. He'd hired an attorney, she just knew it. And she wasn't ready. But she went with him to the bench, facing the ocean, its back to the tourists mingling around. A place for quiet meditation in the midst of activity.

"So, what's up?" he asked, sitting far enough away that they weren't touching, but close enough that she could count his eyelashes when he turned to look at her.

"No," she said. "You first." Divorce details were far more important than past feelings.

"I wanted to ask your opinion on something," he said,

as though he was unsure of his reception. Another first for them.

"Of course."

"I've been given the option to take an early honorable discharge," he said, looking out to sea as he explained the details.

A discharge? But Winston was career navy. It's all he'd ever talked about wanting. Going to college and entering the navy. To have them coming to him with talk of discharge, after he'd been so loyal...

She couldn't believe they'd do that to him. There had to be someone she could talk to. As his wife, shouldn't she have some...

What?

Like the government was going to listen to her? And what would she tell them? That she was divorcing him but that they should definitely keep him on?

"Do you have to take it?" she asked when her thoughts cleared a bit.

"No."

Okay, then. So it was an offer, he'd turn it down, and life would go on as usual.

She looked at him. "Why are you talking to me about it?"

"I've been thinking about the child."

He was confusing her. She didn't like it. Not when her view of life was still so new and tenuous.

"What about him?"

"He needs to learn about loyalty. Duty. Protecting others."

Her breath came in short little drags of sea air. She had no words.

"There are many things I can't give him," Winston

continued, his face stoic as he looked out at the unending waters he'd always said he loved. "But I can teach him those things. They're my strengths." He turned to look at her as he finished, as though he was waiting for an answer.

But…was there a question in there? What did he want her to say?

In their old life, she'd have known what he needed, almost as though she could think *through* him. In the olden days she'd have asked what he thought he couldn't give, because she'd have firmly believed that there was nothing their child would need that he couldn't provide. And conversely, if he couldn't provide it, their child wouldn't need it.

The olden days were gone. She thought about what the man sitting beside her had just told her.

"Are you thinking about leaving the navy because of Tristan?" she asked, not quite sure what to make of that. On any level.

"I want to know what you think about the possibility of me going with NCIS. Or even local police."

"Not local police," she said instantly. Winston knew and loved ships. Every single twist and turn in every single belly of them.

"NCIS has an office in LA. I'd have to be gone for a few months of training, in Georgia, but I could put in a request to work out of the LA office, and I've been told that I stand a good chance of having my request granted."

He wanted to stick around to be an active participant in their son's life! That's what he was telling her! How could she possibly, in that moment, focus on anything else?

A miracle was happening in the midst of everything else falling apart.

He was waiting for her to say something. Something pertinent, preferably.

"Would it be anything like the television show where you'd still be working on ships occasionally? In an investigative capacity?" Winston loved the ships.

"Yes. But truthfully, Em, I'm more into the whole law enforcement/protection part of things now than I am the sailing. I loved it while I did it, but after Afghanistan, I want to use my skills differently."

"Then by all means, go for it!"

He looked at her. "You really mean that?"

Holding his gaze, she nodded. "I do."

He wanted to be close to his son. She just couldn't believe it. And yet…in the midst of all the turmoil something settled deep inside her.

Chapter Twenty

So, hell. Maybe Adamson had been right about talking to Em about his career future. His choices still affected her because of the child if nothing else, even though they were no longer together.

It was good to see her, too. To know that she was taking care of herself. He couldn't tell if her stomach had grown any—she was wearing uncharacteristically loose clothing. But based on that, he had an idea that she was going to be a particularly sexy pregnant woman. She looked as fine in loose clothes and flip-flops as she did in tight skirts and heels.

He was glad she'd called, suggested they get together.

There were other things to talk to her about, like when she wanted to see lawyers and get his things out of her house, but maybe this was an instance where Time still had work to do. Their split was still so raw, the realization that their love had been a fantasy was years old to him, but brand-new to her.

"What did you want to talk to me about?" he asked, not wanting the silence to get awkward on them.

"I need to know something." She was looking at her flip-flops.

"I told you I'd tell you anything I could," he reminded.

"In the past—well, up until two weeks ago from four tomorrow morning—I really believed that we were this special couple. Singled out, chosen, by God or whatever powers that be, to be together. All the plans we made as kids, the vows…that was weird, you know. Most kids don't do that. And here we were, both of us, wanting all the same things and talking about them, too. I thought it was predestined, and that with all that, as long as we went along with destiny—got married, followed the plan—that we'd be protected. That you'd get orders and leave, but always come back to me. I didn't have to worry about it. I just knew. And when you came back, I'd be here healthy and happy and waiting for you. Even when we had trouble getting pregnant and I was looking at my age and knowing that four kids might become a stretch for us, I just figured that the universe knew better. That if I had to have a baby at forty, we'd be protected and that baby would be born healthy. Our love was that strong. That special."

"You had to know at some point it would end." He told her what he knew. "No one lives forever."

"I thought we'd die of old age, within hours or days of each other, when both of us felt as though we'd had complete lives. When we were ready."

He couldn't speak to that. Wasn't really sure what she wanted from him.

"I need to know what you believed, Win."

Her voice was a thread.

"I don't know," he said. He knew what she'd described was a dangerous fantasy.

"Back then, when we talked about all that stuff, were you just humoring me?"

"Of course not."

"So…did you believe it, too?"

"No" was on the tip of his tongue. Until he looked at her.

She needed his truth.

No matter how much it hurt.

"Yes."

The following Friday Winston called Emily, said he had a favor to ask her, asked if he could come into town, maybe pick up a few things. She'd had a long week at work, a good successful week, a lot of late days, was hungry and tired, but of course she said yes.

They were going to have to talk about the divorce. He needed to be able to get a place of his own. She figured, as she wandered through her house alone every morning and night, she was getting more used to the idea. Funny how time really did take care of things sometimes.

The fantasy of youth was dying.

She was all grown up.

And was hoping that she and Win could stay good friends. The phone calls they'd been sharing back and forth, just to check in, were nice. She'd been slowly starting to talk about her business deals with him, her clients, discussing strategies as she had in the past. He had a way of getting to the heart of the matter. Or asking questions that got her there. She trusted his judgment.

He was talking to her, too, at least more than he had been. Had already applied and been accepted to the CITP, the NCIS criminal investigators training program, in Glynco, Georgia. His first step for becoming a special agent. It was a fifty-six-day program, followed by the Special Agent Basic Training Program for another forty-some days. He had to go when classes were offered, and wanted to get it done before she delivered, if possible.

Military wives often gave birth with their husbands off on deployment, and she wouldn't even be his wife anymore by the time Tristan came, but she loved that he was factoring them into his plans.

That Tristan was going to know his father.

He offered to take her out to dinner—anywhere she wanted to go—which would probably have been the best for them, keep things more impersonal. But she just wanted to be home where she could change into sweats and have bare feet. He said he'd pick something up and meet there.

She'd hardly had a chance to get out of her skirt and jacket and into a pair of leggings and a loose T-shirt before he was knocking on the door. The front door.

"Why didn't you pull into the garage?" she asked, wondering if she'd taken up more than her fair share of space. She'd been pulling in without his car there for a couple of weeks now; she could be getting sloppy.

He shrugged. She glanced at the front doorknob. "Or use your key?"

His gaze met hers. No words were exchanged, but she got his answer. Her house wasn't his anymore. He was respecting her space.

"That's nuts, Winston," she said, more acerbic than normal. She'd had that long week. And was four months pregnant. "We both own this home. And it's your son's home, too." Her argument rang a little weak, so she continued, as she walked toward the dining room. "Once we figure out what's happening, we might end up selling the place to split the proceeds," she added.

"You're thinking about moving?"

She hadn't been. But...

"Would you want to live in the home we bought together? Set up together? Lived in together?"

All of those things had been part of the comfort the home had brought her while he'd been gone. But knowing that it had all been a fairy tale...

"But we just did the nursery."

There was that. She was tired. And hungry. So she pulled one of his moves and just shrugged.

He'd brought Mexican food—one of her favorites— but as he was pulling the various covered tin pans out of the bag, he stopped and looked at her. "I didn't think. Is this going to be too spicy for you?"

His thoughtfulness, such a Winston thing, brought tears to her eyes. She reached for glasses as she told him, "Nope! Tristan loves Mexican as much as I do."

If he was there to ask her for the divorce, she hoped he waited until after they ate. She'd given the settlement some thought. As far as she was concerned, he was entitled to half of everything. Her one caveat was that she didn't want to fight about it.

Wasn't going to fight about it.

She'd rather walk away with nothing than get in a court battle with Winston.

"I mentioned I have a favor to ask," he said as they finished up the last of the tamales he'd brought. There'd be some enchilada left over. She'd eaten most of the beans, but limited herself on the rice. She'd read about potential rice risks to pregnant women if they ate too much of it. How much was too much? One never really knew when reading all of the opinion pieces out there.

"Em?"

She didn't want to talk about the divorce, and what other favor would he ask of her at this point? Except to give him the freedom he'd wanted since he'd come home?

"Yeah?"

"I need to take a trip to Wisconsin. To see someone. I'd like to know if you'd consider going with me."

She listened to his words, watched the expressions chase across his face. Regret. Guilt. Compassion. None of it computed.

Who did he know in Wisconsin? Why would he want her to go? Especially with them divorcing. Unless it had to do with the divorce? Did he know an attorney in Wisconsin? Someone he met when he was away from her? Would a Wisconsin attorney be certified in California? Possible if the guy had been military and stationed in San Diego for a time…

Winston wanted her to go on a trip with him?

"When?"

"At your convenience."

She stared at him. Her answer seemed to matter to him. Or going did. Or both.

"What's going on?"

He glanced toward the backyard, not that much was visible in the darkness, and then back at her. "It's been brought to my attention that it's possible I used Danny, changed identities with him, because it allowed me to do what had to be done."

It wasn't about the divorce.

As she gazed into those troubled eyes, she felt his struggle. Knew a sense of fullness, a depth of completion she hadn't known she'd been missing. She was feeling him again. Not just knowing him, but actually feeling. Her heart became his, or felt his so completely it seemed like they'd become joined. She got up from the table so abruptly she hit her knee. Ignored the searing pain as she carried trash, leftovers and dishes to the sink. She just needed a minute. Time to get out of fantasy and into reality.

It had happened so fast, falling back into the fairy tale. No warning. She'd had no idea it could even happen, now that she knew it wasn't real.

Reality.

Winston carried in the glasses. Was right behind her. Turning, she looked up at him, in blue jeans and a striped button-up shirt, the cuffs rolled a couple of times.

Taking his hand, she led them to the living room. To the couch. Sat down—no longer touching at all.

"Tell me," she said, hoping she had herself firmly in check again.

"He was single. Not even a serious girlfriend. He'd made no promises to anyone other than the United States government when he was sworn in as a soldier."

He meant that Danny could give up his life and be the hero without being unfaithful to his personal self. It was as though the words were in Winston's brain and wirelessly streamed to hers.

"By becoming him, it was almost as though Winston Hannigan died that day in the desert, with a change of clothes," she said aloud, staring at him.

He shrugged, as though not quite going that far with it.

"I need to go see his parents," Winston said, while she

was busy grappling with the emotions barreling through her. From hope to despair and everything in between.

"I need to tell them that their son died a hero, that I was with him in the end. I have to apologize to them for giving up their son's body. For robbing them of the chance to bury him."

The trip to Wisconsin. She didn't even question the fact that he wanted her to go. She and Winston always stood by each other through the difficult times in life. Their grandparents' funerals. Her father's funeral. Even before they were lovers, they'd stood side by side, taking on the tough stuff. It's what best friends did.

"I'd like you to be there, Em. I want them to see why I did what I did. Not because I deserve their forgiveness, but because I hope it will help ease their pain. To know that I needed their son to get the job done."

"Of course I'm going with you," she said, sitting there with him as platonic as they'd ever been. "And not just for them, Winston," she added, then got up and went in to finish cleaning away dinner.

She couldn't keep sitting there looking at him. It confused her. He confused her.

Her feelings confused her.

She was a thirty-three-year-old fully-grown woman who couldn't decipher between real emotion and make-believe.

Or maybe it was just the pregnancy hormones.

Chapter Twenty-One

She sat by the window. He took the middle seat. It was a routine they'd established many years before, during innumerable vacations they'd taken together. It used to be that she'd offer to take the middle, her being the smaller of the two of them, but each time he'd insisted on his place. Flying was a no-brainer for him. Didn't faze him. Emily got a little claustrophobic now and then. Didn't like not being in control. Focusing out the window made her feel not so closed in.

The middle seat allowed him to go either direction to protect her. That's all it had ever been about for him. Protecting her. His feisty friend who saw herself as the person least in the need of protection. Truth was, he knew she didn't need his protection. He just had always needed to make sure that if she ever did, he'd be there.

Until he'd chosen to turn his back on her needs to protect his comrades.

He'd made that choice the day he joined up. He knew that now. Maybe she'd known, too. Adamson had suggested as much. Said he gave Emily too little credit.

Funny, he'd always thought he gave her more credit than he'd ever given himself.

He'd called ahead to make the Sunday appointment with the Garrisons, who came outside to greet him and Emily when he pulled the rental car into their driveway, a week and two days after he'd asked Emily to accompany him to Milwaukee. Mrs. Garrison—Clara, she told them to call her—had made a peach pastry from scratch and offered them coffee to go with it. Then looked at Emily's slightly protruding belly, looked at her husband and smiled, offering to brew some tea.

He was surprised by her insight. His soon-to-be ex-wife looked pregnant to him, because he knew her body almost as well as he knew his own, and because he knew she was pregnant. But to someone who didn't know her, she could just be a little paunchy—in the one area. She'd worn a dress, black, plain, three-quarter-length sleeves, a few inches above the knees, and stretchy. It was her funeral dress. He'd worn dress blues.

Harold Garrison led them out to a screened porch looking over a modest though nicely maintained backyard. All of the plants were little more than sticks in the fall weather, but he imagined they were quite colorful during the spring and summer. They surrounded a fountain that made a tinkling sound as water fell from one layer down to the next, ending in an oblong-shaped pool in the ground.

"Harold and Danny built that together," Clara said. "It used to have fish in it. Danny wanted a fish tank. A simple fish tank. He got a pond." Shaking her head, Clara was also smiling as she told her story.

Area heaters warmed the chilly sixty-degree outside air.

"I was hoping it would be warm enough for us to sit out here," Clara said.

"I told her it would be," Harold chimed in. "She worries, you know, but I'd looked at the Doppler."

"He did tell me, and I do worry." The room was outfitted with dark wicker furniture—couch, rockers, chairs and tables. The couple showed them to a glass-topped outdoor table with four chairs on the other end of the room. Clara put down the pastry. Harold followed her up with plates, forks, napkins and a serving utensil. They both went back for the cups of coffee and tea.

Tense, almost wishing the couple were a bit less hospitable considering what he had to tell them, Winston pulled out a wicker-back chair for Emily and then took his own seat next to her. Her knee touched his under the table. It could have been by accident.

But he believed it was on purpose.

"Maybe I should just leave them to their peace," he said softly, head down.

"I know you said you came to apologize," she replied, equally soft. "But you know you're really here to bring them closure. To let them know about Danny's last hours so they aren't always wondering. The doubts, the not knowing, can cripple you."

He looked at her. Reminded of a time when they'd been in high school, looking at colleges, and he'd been wrestling with the idea of becoming a businessman—real estate, like his father. He'd have made a lot of money following in his father's footsteps. Could have taken over his small but successful and reputable Marie Cove bro-

kerage from him. Emily had listened to all of his reasons
for going the business route—something everyone had
always expected he would do—and then calmly asked
why he'd do such a thing when all he'd ever wanted was
to sail for his country?

At that point, he'd never mentioned to her that he'd seriously wondered about joining the navy. He hadn't told
anyone. Taking over for his father had just been assumed.
He was an only child. There was no one else.

"What?" she asked, bringing to his attention that he
was staring at her. Before he could answer, the Garrisons
were back, taking a seat.

Why was it that so often, when people met to talk,
food was included? Didn't folks get that some conversations made eating difficult?

Emily's knee touched his under the table again. He
ate. Listened as Clara regaled them with stories from
Danny's youth. Always coming back to the fact that he'd
been looking out for the underdog his entire life. From
pet rescue—he had to take the one that wasn't cute—to
kids in school who got bullied. The more she talked, with
Harold sometimes completing her sentence or story, the
worse Winston felt for them.

Danny was all they'd had.

When silence fell, more than an hour later, half the
pastry still sitting uneaten on the platter in the middle
of the table, coffee cups empty, Winston sat up straight,
his back firmly against his chair.

"I came to tell you that I was with your son..." He
paused, blinked. Swallowed. Pressed his leg against
Emily's. "I was with him before the ambush. We ate
together." He could remember their last conversation—
Danny had asked Winston about being away from Emily

for so long at a time, a conversation he might share with others someday. "I saw him get hit."

He looked them both in the eye. They deserved that. Their tears ripped at his insides.

"I can attest to you, with utter honesty, that Danny died protecting the troops with whom he served. He died without fear. He died with honor."

There was protocol. Things that were said to immediate family by the military, when they were informed about a loved one's death. This wasn't that.

The Garrisons had had that visit.

He didn't look at Emily. But he felt her there. Not just her knee. He knew she was looking at him, not Danny's parents.

"Thank you, son," Harold said, lips and chin quivering. "You have no idea what it means to us, that you'd take the time to come see us on his behalf…"

Winston nodded. "I have to tell you as well that it is my fault that Danny's body didn't make it back to you. But I hope that in knowing the truth, you'll appreciate that your son's last, posthumous act is still saving lives today."

Where those words came from, he didn't know. They just showed up and shot out of his mouth.

He told them about his rogue plan. About changing identities with Danny in the desert that god-awful day. How he'd left Danny sitting up by a tree because sitting up against a tree was something he'd seen his comrade do at the end of a good day. And how, when he'd been forced to show his loyalty to the militants with whom he'd lived, he'd shot at Danny's body from a distance, making it look as though he'd killed a living US soldier.

"I delivered his body to them," he said. "He ended up in a burn pit with other US soldiers who died during that skirmish." What the fiends had done to him first was between them and God—with Winston as a witness to horrors he would never forget. "I visited that grave every chance I got," he said, and then, breaking eye contact with them, he bowed his head.

In shame. In regret.

For war. For things that had to be.

For not coming up with a better plan. Emily softly touched his thigh under the table. He'd forgotten for a second that she was there.

And that he wasn't done.

"It was recently brought to my attention, by my therapist," he admitted with difficulty, "that perhaps the reason I chose to use Danny's body was because it made me capable of completing the mission," he continued. "Danny was unattached—other than the two of you." He lowered his head toward them and then forced himself to finish. "He'd made a promise to protect his country, even if that meant giving up his life. I'd done the same, but I'd also made a promise to my wife—that I would come back to her. The theory is that in my mind, I died in the desert that day. And with Danny's persona, the strength I'd known him to have, with his identity, I was able to complete my mission."

"Do you believe in fate, Officer Hannigan?" Clara's voice brought his head up.

Her gaze was so hopeful, he almost nodded. He couldn't lie to her. "Unfortunately, no."

"No matter," she said to him, looking at Harold, who nodded. "Because God doesn't rely on us to put fate to work for us. She's busy on our behalves all the time, whether we know, or believe, or not."

Emily pulled away. Not so that anyone but him noticed, probably. But he felt her withdrawal.

Understood it. They were on the same page again for a moment. They both had learned the dangers in believing in those ethereal dreams. Finding out that "Santa Claus" wasn't real had devastated her. And knocked him for a bit of a loop, too.

Clara wiped her eyes, a tissue balled in the palm of her hand, while Harold put his arm around her, patting her shoulder.

"There's no mistake in the fact that you sat Danny up against that tree. No mistake that you'd seen him sit that way at the end of the day, prompting you to leave him that way at the end of his last day," she continued, while Harold patted a little more quickly.

"That was fate," Harold said. "She designed it all. Just as, I'm certain, it was her design that put you and Danny in the same unit."

Talk about kidding yourself with a load of fantasy.

But he couldn't blame them. Or point out their error. What did it hurt to leave them believing? Who'd be hurt by it? Certainly not this older couple who'd just lost their only child.

"You don't believe us," Clara said, looking from him to Emily and back again.

Emily sniffed, grabbed another tissue, but remained as silent beside him as she'd been since he'd begun.

Reaching behind her, Clara grabbed a pile of letters from a little metal plant stand in the corner.

He recognized the markings. They were military letters, from Afghanistan.

"Our son wrote to us about you," Harold said, glancing down at those letters. "About both of you." He nodded toward Emily and watched as Clara opened the top envelope.

Staring at those envelopes, knowing he'd been with Danny when he'd mailed most of them, had watched the young man writing some of them, Winston wanted to get up and head home. He hadn't expected...

The day had been destined for difficult, but this was...

"'I know you were worried when I left, Mom, but my whole life, you've talked to me about listening to the still, small voice inside. You've told me that as long as I follow that voice, trust it, my life will be what it is meant to be. That I will reach my true potential and do what I am meant to do...'"

Clara's voice broke... Winston swallowed. For Danny, because he knew the soldier would want Winston to tend to his parents, Winston remained seated even though all he wanted was to get away. A barrier settled around him, similar to the one that had coated him in the desert the day he'd struck out on his own. And for the two years he'd been in captivity.

Emily sniffed. Grabbed yet another tissue.

Harold patted.

"'I met someone over here, Mom. He reminds me of you and Dad more than anyone I've ever met. He's got this wife...they've been together since they were fourteen...just like you and Dad. They grew up in the same small town, but met when they started high school, just like the two of you...'" Clara's voice broke.

Emily's breathing was erratic.

"'He talks about how they just knew...how they planned their whole lives...'" Clara continued, crying openly now. "'He proposed when they were fifteen, just like Dad did. He says that some people are just predestined to be together, like some are predestined to be heroes on the football field, or the battle field…'" She sniffled, caught her breath on a sob, blinked. "'…or be millionaires.'"

Harold took the letter from her shaking fingers.

"'Their grandparents died while they were in high school, and her father died, too, just like Grandpa Chambers,'" Harold continued. "'His parents wanted him to follow his father into real estate, but he had to be a sailor, to join the military…'"

Looking up over a pair of reading glasses, Harold eyed Winston, his wet lashes taking nothing from the sternness of that look. "My father was a farmer," he explained, putting the letter down for a moment. "A damned successful one. I was his only child and had been working the farm since I was old enough to ride on his lap on the tractor. But I wanted to be a police officer."

Okay, this was getting downright eerie. He'd met people with whom he had things in common, but…

"Danny never said anything."

He wanted to read the letter for himself. And didn't at the same time.

"'They want four kids, when you guys only wanted one, but then I was such a great one, who'd want more, right?'" Harold read, doing some sniffling of his own.

And then, looking at the paper in his hand, read, "'I know I'm here to protect him, Mom, to see that he keeps his promise to his wife and gets back home to her…'"

Harold stopped. Clara and Emily were both crying.

And Winston broke.

Chapter Twenty-Two

They had a late-afternoon flight out of Milwaukee back to LA. Emily was just as happy to honor Winston's seeming need for silence as they went about the business of traveling. Getting through security, boarding, landing, remembering where he'd parked his car in the garage early that morning, heading back to Marie Cove.

She had to work the next morning. He had appointments at the base, but not until later in the day.

"Why don't you just stay here?" she asked him, weary beyond her means, as he pulled into the driveway of their home. He put the car in Park, but didn't turn it off.

"Please, Winston. I won't read more into it than is there. It's late. I don't want to worry about you driving home after the day we've had. And… I don't… Please, I just kind of need you close tonight."

He still didn't open the garage door. But he shut off the ignition. And walked with her to the front door.

Told her to go ahead and head to bed since she had to be up early in the morning.

"You're coming in, right?" she asked him.

He hesitated, but then nodded, and she went down the hall to the suite that had started out as theirs. And now was just hers.

The Garrisons' story, it had been nice. Okay, incredibly beautiful.

There'd been some pretty impressive coincidences between Harold's and Winston's lives.

But that didn't mean Winston and Emily had what it took to make a marriage work in the real world. Not without the fantasy holding them together.

So it was a bit...confusing, that part about Clara teaching Danny that some lives are predestined to certain paths and mentioning couples...but that's what made fairy tales fairy tales, right?

The fact that they contained things everyone wanted to believe.

And it's what made fairy tales live from person to person, generation to generation, country to country—people's need to believe in something bigger than what they had.

Still...

Clara and Harold were incredibly lucky.

As had become habit since Winston came home, she climbed into bed before he came into the room, leaving the bathroom light on for him. It was too late for television. She had to be up in six hours. And had been halfway across the country and back since she'd last slept.

Had she been alone, she might have dropped right off. As it was, she lay there, listening. Waiting. While he'd been appropriately moved in front of the Garrisons earlier in the day, Winston had been fairly tight-lipped since they'd left the other couple's house.

Getting on the right road, dealing with traffic and getting back to the airport had consumed those first minutes. And then getting through security in time to catch their flight. Then there'd been the woman sitting in the aisle seat, preventing any real conversation between them. She'd figured him for as exhausted as she was in the drive home from the LA airport.

Too tired to deal with any of it.

She heard him in the office. Opening a drawer. Figured maybe he had another thing or two to pick up. The hall light went out and he was there, in the bedroom with her.

He made short work of the bathroom, grabbing a toothbrush out of the stash of extras—dentist giveaways—that she kept on a shelf in the closet. A cool breeze hit her skin as the covers lifted. The mattress dipped and Emily closed her eyes.

She woke up an hour or so later, with Winston spooned behind her. Not holding her. Just close. Turning over, she put an arm around his waist and he rolled to his back, sliding his arm beneath her shoulders. Settling her head on his chest, with his arm around her waist, her whole body pressed against him down to their feet, she went back to sleep.

Winston was awake when Emily got up and showered in the morning. Dressing in fresh clothes from his closet—some he'd left until he had more space—he went in to make her tea and get her vitamins down out of the cupboard they'd appeared in a couple of months ago. When she came into the kitchen, dressed in navy pants and a loose-fitting blouse beneath a cropped jacket, he asked her how she was feeling.

And told her he'd lock up behind her as she left.

He didn't tell her he'd be there when she got back.

She didn't ask, either.

He figured they both knew he wouldn't be.

Winston got the call from Emily at nine thirty that morning. There was an active shooter not far from her office building just south of LA. Six miles, actually, but if he wasn't caught, a guy could travel six miles in a number of minutes.

"Stay down, away from all windows," he told her, grabbing his keys. Thank God he was still at their house when she'd called. He was halfway there already. "And stay inside," he added, out the front door and heading toward the car. "I mean it, Em. Don't go outside, for any reason."

Bullets ricocheted and there was no predicting the path they'd take.

"Winston, I'm fine," she said. "You don't need to come. No one has been hurt, thank God. It's a kid from the high school. They have him cornered, he's just not in custody yet. I just wanted you to know, in case you heard something on the news, that it's all okay."

He'd heard her the first time.

"I'm on my way," he told her.

"There's nothing for you to do here."

He knew that. He wasn't losing his mind. But he wasn't going to lose anything more, either.

"I'd like to take you to lunch," he said, thinking on the fly. "Do you have time to go to lunch?" He was heading toward the freeway entrance ramp, easily ten miles over the speed limit.

"Of course. I have to eat."

"I didn't know if you had a business lunch planned."

"Not today."

Yeah, fate had a way of controlling things that way when she chose to do so.

He might be stubborn, and a bit too fond of being in charge, but he wasn't completely dense. There was too much piling up for him to be able to continue existing in the emotional freezer he'd somehow built for himself-calling it reality. Because he couldn't keep pretending he was unaffected. The reality was…he hurt so bad he didn't know how to handle it. And so he hadn't.

Danny had been willing to die to give him and Emily this chance. And her… She'd lived life every day with her heart open and hurting to keep them together.

And what had he done? He'd gone into hiding in the name of being a soldier.

Emily had been the strong one, hanging on to what mattered most, fighting the hardest fight, while he'd been the coward, hiding away in his safe lonely place.

It was a place he didn't want to leave. Had planned to remain untouched for the rest of his life.

And as much as he wished to God he could stay there, guaranteed not to hurt anymore, he also needed desperately to be free. Free to love his wife. And his son.

It was time to be the soldier he'd thought he was.

Trouble was, he'd shattered Emily's ability to believe in the miracle of love and had no idea in hell how to turn things around.

He was a soldier on the most important mission of his life and he had no plan.

"So hear this, Mrs. Fate," he said aloud as he sped toward the only woman who'd ever held the position of wife in his heart, the only one he'd ever wanted. "You brought us together. You brought me home to her. This one's on you. I hope to God you've got a plan."

Emily walked out of the lobby to meet Winston when he strode up. He'd scared the bejesus out of her, high-tailing it to LA when there was no reason to do so.

He looked perfectly normal, and sounded that way, too, as he said hello and asked her where she wanted to eat.

If it weren't for the baby growing so voraciously inside her, she wouldn't have wanted to eat. She opted for a row of food trucks in a park nearby so they could sit outside. She needed a good dose of serotonin. Something scientific that she could rely on to raise her spirits a bit.

His khakis, an older pair, she could tell by the fade in the fabric, were freshly pressed, down to the cuffs on the sleeves. He looked good, a sailor among the business-people milling about. Reminding her of a song she'd once loved by the Dixie Chicks about a soldier shipping out, and a young girl waiting for him, even though everyone told her he was too old for her.

The song had ended sadly. But what had spoken to her about that song was how that young girl had recognized real love. How she'd seen the soldier and just known. And then hadn't let anyone convince her differently.

That was real love, she'd thought. The song ended badly because the soldier died. Not because love had.

They got wraps. Sat at a scarred and splintery picnic table to eat them. Talked about the people coming and going. Imaging their business, where they were off to, what they were thinking. Playing a game they used to play when they were kids on a date at the beach, with each scenario getting just a little bit more ridiculous than the last. When he started talking about an older woman who he claimed had just come from skinny-dipping on the beach with her twenty-five-year-old lover, someone too exhausted to keep up with her, which was why he wasn't in sight, she burst out laughing.

He stared at her. She stared back.

"I haven't heard you laugh in..."

Not since he'd been back. Not any real laughter.

Real.

"You scared me earlier," she said. "Rushing up here, talking about windows and bullets..."

He shrugged. "So I'm still a bit shell-shocked from my time in the desert," he acknowledged. "I was also just scared senseless at the thought of losing you before..."

"Before what?"

He shrugged again. "I was just heading back to the base when you called," he told her. "But then you knew that I would be, didn't you? Knew that I wouldn't be at the house when you got home tonight?"

She nodded. Not sure where he was going with all of this.

"Before what?"

He shook his head. "Not here." After clearing up their trash, he tossed it several feet into a can. Made the basket, just as he always did.

She'd once told him he should play basketball. He'd told her, way back then, that he was made for more serious pursuits. She'd thought, at the time, that he'd meant he wanted to spend all of his time with her, not practicing on the court.

"You mind if I stay at the house one more night so we can talk?" he asked as they headed back up the street toward her office. "I can pick up some steaks."

He probably wanted to talk about the divorce.

She was trying to watch her red meat intake, but protein was good for the baby.

"That sounds good," she told him, and was surprised that the pain mixed in there, wasn't debilitating her.

Maybe they really would find a way to be friends forever.

He knew where the candles were. The china Emily had insisted he help choose when they registered for their wedding. He found a decent tablecloth. And did a little cleaning, too, to fill the place with the lavender scent that was now showing up everywhere in the house—even the cleaning fluids.

He'd changed out of his khakis into the black jeans and pullover shirt that had been Emily's favorites, way back when. She'd purchased them for him the Christmas before he'd left for ground training.

He thought about changing the sheets, too, but didn't want to give her the wrong impression. This wasn't a seduction he was setting up.

As hungry as his body had grown for his wife's, he'd tamp down those urges forever if it meant he got to be in her life for that long.

By the time she got home, he'd worked himself into a bit of a manic state, completely unlike the man he'd ever been—before or after the desert.

It wasn't a seduction plan. He knew that much. But what kind of plan was it?

Fate wasn't being kind to him—not so that he could

see, at any rate. He was presenting himself, standing front and center in the midst of the mess he'd made, trusting her to come up with a plan.

Emily pulled into the garage, and he had nothing but steaks on the grill and a salad in the fridge. She changed, into the leggings and loose comfortable shirt that had apparently become her new at-home wardrobe.

Maybe someone—him—should take her shopping for some maternity clothes. With nothing else coming to him, he suggested as much over his candlelit steak dinner that was going nowhere, solving nothing, with no goal in mind and what could only be billed as a failed mission.

"I don't want to spend a bunch of money on clothes I'm only going to wear for a few months," she told him. "I really think I'll be able to get through most of this with just leggings. Plus, they're really comfortable."

The failed suggestion pretty much fit the rest of the mission. So much for fate.

"If I were going to have more kids, you know, like we'd originally thought, then, yeah, I've seen some cute things I might be tempted to buy, but as it is…"

"Do you want more kids?" What the hell? They'd known since they were fifteen that they wanted four. They'd each written down the number on a piece of paper, not showing the other, and had both written the same number.

And now here he was talking to her like he didn't know that?

He dropped his fork. Stared at her. She wasn't eating much. Had her napkin in both hands, just holding it. And was looking right back at him.

"We…were something, weren't we?" he asked, trying

to get them out of the hell into which he'd just inadvertently plummeted them.

"Yes, we were."

He'd gone for levity. Her tone was as serious as his had been. Another fail.

It was time to be Winston Hannigan. A soldier. A man who put his life on the line for what mattered most.

"I think it's possible that we still are," he told her.

Hands clearly shaking, she put her napkin on her plate. "Oh, Winston, let's not go there…"

"I'm not going, Em," he told her. "I *am* there. Truth is, I don't think I ever left. I shut down. But I never left." Listening to Danny's letter the day before had completely crushed the barrier that putting on the soldier's clothes had given him. Stripped him bare to the nude, determined but frightened man he'd been that day in the desert when he'd changed clothes on his way to turning himself in to the enemy.

Tears in her eyes, she pushed away from the table. Shaking her head. "It's too late, Winston. I sat around here for months, waiting, and…it's too late."

It had to be because of Afsoon. The one thing he'd known would break them. It wasn't something he could undo.

He could never return to being the man who knew the feel of only his wife's body wrapped around him.

Armed with that knowledge, the plan became clear. He even understood now why fate had left him hanging high and dry. He had to go.

Had to do what he'd been telling himself all along.

Had to leave her to find a man with whom she could be happy. Where old vows didn't haunt her. And new ones would be keepable. And kept.

Gathering his keys, he headed toward the door.

"Where in the hell do you think you're going?"

Her words stopped him in his tracks. He noticed a new, somewhat shrill tone come to her voice a time or two since she'd become pregnant. It had reached new levels.

"You think you're ever going to walk out on me again, Winston Hannigan, you just better think again."

He turned around. "But...you said..."

"I said it's too late for me to be back where we were," she said. "I didn't say give up and walk out the door before we could figure out what or where that leaves us."

There was sense in that. He heard it. But more, he heard the sense in his own brain that was telling him to sit back down and wait.

He followed orders.

"So..." She sat back down, picked up her knife and fork, cut a piece of what had to be cold steak, and ate it. "Where does that leave us?" she asked.

He wasn't sure if the question was rhetorical or if he was supposed to come up with an answer. The way she'd asked, and was paying more attention to eating...

After another couple of bites, she pushed her plate away. "Where does that leave us?" she repeated.

He'd had a better chance of coming up with a plan in the desert. He couldn't think straight, with her sitting there, giving him a chance to have a life with her again.

He remembered being fourteen, tripping over himself to get to her every day. Afraid to say something she'd think stupid and have her move on to the next guy. He'd told her so. She said she'd been feeling the exact same way about him. They'd talked for hours.

Become best friends.

Forever.

"I think we were right, Em. I think that some couples are predestined to be together. I think Clara and Harold are like that, too. Some souls, they leave wherever they came from, with a connection so close there that they have to live this life together."

She teared up. And shook her head.

"But I think we were wrong to think that that connection was protected. That it would keep us safe from whatever challenges life gave us. I might die too young, Em. Or you might. We might not be able to have a second child, let alone four. I'm called to put my life on the line, to protect others, whether I'm a solider, a special agent or something else. I have to risk my life. But it doesn't mean that my heart is anywhere—first, foremost and always—other than right here with you. That's what I think."

Tears flowed down her cheeks. She was shaking her head.

He'd put it all on the line. Had nothing else.

Except.

"I love you, Emily. Every moment of every day since the second I met you, I've loved you. I can promise you that. I loved you so much I changed clothes with another soldier. And when I was with Afsoon—" he had to get it out there, whether he lost her or not "—the only way I could get my body to respond was to close my eyes and think of you. You asked me how it was with her. Truth is… I have no idea. I was so far into you, pretending I was lying with you, remembering you, that I have no idea how she felt…"

Sobbing, Emily reached out her arms to him and Winston realized he needed no plan. He picked her up, even had sense about him to blow out the candles, and took her back to their room, to their bed, to hold her until they could both start to believe that they had each other back.

That the war was over.

At least for them.

"I love you so much, Winston. This morning, when you came racing up like that, I was so scared you were losing it. I'm scared to death of losing you. I know what it feels like now and I just... But...living without you is even worse."

"You were okay, Em. Sad. Lonely. But you were okay. You had the strength of my love, I see that now. As I had yours. Our love gave me the strength to survive, and it did the same for you, too, you know. You took our love to the fertility clinic and made a life that would make you happy. That's what finally came to me. Our love is real, Em. It's so real its strength continues even if our physical bodies don't. That's what the Garrisons know. And why they're still okay, even with Danny gone. Because the love doesn't leave. It never will. Ever."

He held her while she cried. He cried some, too. They talked a lot. He told her how petrified he'd been when she'd first mentioned an active shooter that morning. About all the nights in the desert when he had lain not sleeping, able to stay awake because those were the hours he could spend with her uninterrupted. How he'd suddenly remember little moments that had long been forgotten.

And then they made love. Long, slow, tender love that ended with a single thrust home. It was all he had, one thrust, and he exploded inside her. Something else he'd never done with Afsoon—come inside her. Someday he'd share that with Emily, too, but not then.

He didn't want the other woman anywhere near Emily again that night.

He wasn't just imagining Emily's arms. He was in them.

"I was thinking," he said, sometime past three in the morning. They'd yet to sleep. He didn't even feel tired.

"What?" she asked, grinning, as she propped herself up on his chest and looked at him expectantly. His Emily. Always open to whatever he had to say.

"That maybe we should name our baby Danny."

Tears filled her eyes again. "Our baby," she said.

"Our baby," he agreed, his hand reaching down to cup her stomach. "My son."

"Daniel Harold Hannigan," she said, sniffling and smiling. "I love it."

He did, too. And fully believed that Danny would approve, wherever he might be.

Looking around the room, seeing mostly the night's shadows, Winston gave a nod to the powers he couldn't see. Fate was out there, someplace. Working hard to bring happiness to others.

With another silent nod, an inner smile, he saluted her. *Mission accomplished.*

* * * * *

*Check out the next book in
The Parent Portal miniseries,
available January 2020 from
Harlequin Special Edition!*

*And in the meantime, be sure to try
The Daycare Chronicles miniseries:*

Her Lost and Found Baby
An Unexpected Christmas Baby
The Baby Arrangement

*Available now wherever
Harlequin Special Edition books
and ebooks are sold.*

COMING NEXT MONTH FROM

H HARLEQUIN®

SPECIAL EDITION

Available June 18, 2019

#2701 HER FAVORITE MAVERICK
Montana Mavericks: Six Brides for Six Brothers • by Christine Rimmer
Logan Crawford might just be the perfect man. A girl would have to be a fool to turn him down. Or a coward. Sarah Turner thinks she might be both. But the single mom has no time for love. Logan, however, is determined to steal her heart!

#2702 A PROMISE FOR THE TWINS
The Wyoming Multiples • by Melissa Senate
Former soldier Nick Garroway is in Wedlock Creek to fulfill a promise made to a fallen soldier: check in on the woman the man had left pregnant with twins. Brooke Timber is in need of a nanny, so what else can Nick do but fill in? She's also planning his father's wedding, and all the family togetherness soon has Brooke and Nick rethinking if this promise is still worth keeping.

#2703 THE FAMILY HE DIDN'T EXPECT
The Stone Gap Inn • by Shirley Jump
Dylan Millwright's bittersweet homecoming gets a whole lot sweeter when he meets Abby Cooper. But this mother of two is all about "the ties that bind," and Dylan isn't looking for strings to keep him down. But do this bachelor's wandering ways conceal the secretly yearning heart of a family man?

#2704 THE DATING ARRANGEMENT
Something True • by Kerri Carpenter
Is the bride who fell on top of bar owner Jack Wright a sign from above? But event planner Emerson Dewitt isn't actually a bride—much to her mother's perpetual disappointment. Until Jack proposes an arrangement. He'll pose as Emerson's boyfriend in exchange for her help relaunching his business. It's a perfect partnership. Until all that fake dating turns into very real feelings...

#2705 A FATHER FOR HER CHILD
Sutter Creek, Montana • by Laurel Greer
Widow Cadence Grigg is slowly putting her life back together—and raising her infant son. By her side is her late husband's best friend, Zach Cardenas, who can't help his burgeoning feelings for Cadie and her baby boy. Though determined not to fall in love again, Cadie might find that Cupid has other plans for her happily-ever-after...

#2706 MORE THAN ONE NIGHT
Wildfire Ridge • by Heatherly Bell
A one-night stand so incredible, Jill Davis can't forget. Memories so delectable, they sustained Sam Hawker through his final tour. Three years later, Jill is unexpectedly face-to-face with her legendary marine lover. And it's clear their chemistry is like gas and a match. Except Sam is her newest employee. That means hands off, sister! Except maybe...just this once? Ooh-rah!

HSECNM0619

Get 4 FREE REWARDS!

We'll send you 2 FREE Books plus 2 FREE Mystery Gifts.

Harlequin® Special Edition books feature heroines finding the balance between their work life and personal life on the way to finding true love.

FREE Value Over **$20**

---

*Former soldier Nick Garroway is in Wedlock Creek
to fulfill a promise made to a fallen soldier: check in
on the woman the man had left pregnant with twins.
Brooke Timber is in need of a nanny, so what else can
Nick do but fill in? She's planning his father's wedding,
and all the family togetherness soon has Brooke and
Nick rethinking if this promise is still temporary...*

*Read on for a sneak preview of
A Promise for the Twins,
the next great book in Melissa Senate's
The Wyoming Multiples miniseries.*

If the Satler triplets were a definite, adding this client for July
would mean she could take off the first couple weeks of August,
which were always slow for Dream Weddings, and just be with
her twins.

Which would mean needing Nick Garroway as her nanny—
manny—until her regular nanny returned. Leanna could take some
time off herself and start mid-August. Win-win for everyone.

A temporary manny. A necessary temporary manny.

"Well, I've consulted with myself," Brooke said as she put
the phone on the table. "The job is yours. I'll only need help until
August 1. Then I'll take some time off, and Leanna, my regular
nanny, will be ready to come back to work for me."

He nodded. "Sounds good. Oh—and I know your ad called
for hours of nine to one during the week, but I'll make you a
deal. I'll be your around-the-clock nanny, as needed—for room
and board."

She swallowed. "You mean live here?"

"Temporarily. I'd rather not stay with my family. Besides, this way, you can work when you need to, not be boxed into someone else's hours."

Even a part-time nanny was very expensive—more than she could afford—but Brooke had always been grateful that necessity would make her limit her work so that she could spend real time with her babies. Now she'd have as-needed care for the twins without spending a penny.

Once again, she wondered where Nick Garroway had come from. He was like a miracle—and everything Brooke needed right now.

"I think I'm getting the better deal," she said. "But my grandmother always said not to look a gift horse in the mouth." Especially when that gift horse was clearly a workhorse.

"Good. You get what you need and I make good on that promise. Works for both of us."

She glanced at him. He might be gorgeous and sexy, and too capable with a diaper and a stack of dirty dishes, but he wasn't her fantasy in the flesh. He was here because he'd promised her babies' father he'd make sure she and the twins were all right. She had to stop thinking of him as a man—somehow, despite how attracted she was to him on a few different levels. He was her nanny, her *manny*.

But what was sexier than a man saying, "Take a break, I'll handle it. Take that call, I've got the kids. Go rest, I'll load the dishwasher and fold the laundry"?

Nothing was sexier. Which meant Brooke would have to be on guard 24/7.

Because her brain had caught up with her—the hot manny was moving into her house."

Don't miss
A Promise for the Twins *by Melissa Senate,*
available July 2019 wherever
Harlequin® *Special Edition books and ebooks are sold.*

www.Harlequin.com

Looking for more satisfying love stories
with community and family at their core?

Check out **Harlequin® Special Edition**
and **Love Inspired®** books!

New books available every month!

CONNECT WITH US AT:

Facebook.com/groups/HarlequinConnection

 Facebook.com/HarlequinBooks

Twitter.com/HarlequinBooks

Instagram.com/HarlequinBooks

Pinterest.com/HarlequinBooks

ReaderService.com

 HARLEQUIN®

**ROMANCE WHEN
YOU NEED IT**

HFGENRE2018

Love Harlequin romance?

DISCOVER.

Be the first to find out about promotions,
news and exclusive content!

EXPLORE.

Sign up for the Harlequin e-newsletter and
download a free book from any series at
TryHarlequin.com.

CONNECT.

Join our Harlequin community to share
your thoughts and connect with other
romance readers!
Facebook.com/groups/HarlequinConnection

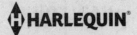

HARLEQUIN®

**ROMANCE WHEN
YOU NEED IT**

HSOCIAL2018